WINNER OF THE STORY PRIZE

LONGLISTED FOR THE JOYCE CAROL OATES PRIZE • ONE OF *TIME'S*
10 BEST FICTION BOOKS OF 2023 AND 100 MU...
A *NEW YORK TIMES BOOK REVIEW* E...

NAMED A BEST BOOK OF TH...

THE NEW YORKER, VANITY FAIR, LI...
ELECTRIC LITERATURE, AND THE NEW YOR... ...

"Absorbing . . . Yoon details fully realized and flawed characters attempting
to wade through the complexities of immigrant life . . . [and] asks urgent
questions about what it really means to belong somewhere."
—*TIME*, The 100 Must-Read Books of 2023

"A slim but exquisite collection . . . that is breathtaking in scope, detailing
the persistence of imperialism, war, poverty, and dislocation across
generations. . . . A masterpiece in restraint . . . Yoon expertly telescopes
between the long view and the close-up."
—MAY-LEE CHAI, *The New York Times*

"In a quietly powerful short story collection, Paul Yoon creates a kaleidoscopic
portrait of the Korean diaspora. In these stories, one of which appeared in
[*The New Yorker*], Yoon's characters struggle to find a place for themselves
in a world where life can be capricious and harsh, but sometimes marked
by grace."
—*THE NEW YORKER*, The Best Books We Read This Week

"Yoon investigates shifting identities and cultures in crisp, low-key writing,
the better to see the stories' ribs."
—*LIBRARY JOURNAL*, Best Short Stories of 2023

"*The Hive and the Honey* comprises seven masterful short stories that span
five hundred years of Korean diaspora. . . . Yoon's grandfather escaped
North Korea, and the author's works deal fittingly with belonging, home,
immigration, and identity." —*TIME*, 15 New Books You Should Read in October

"Yoon's haunting, evocative new collection centers on themes of migration,
displacement, collective memory, and the Korean diaspora."
—*THE NEW YORK TIMES*, 34 Works of Fiction to Read This Fall

"The book is 148 pages of exquisite, subtly interwoven narratives—a brief,
evocative volume perfect for sinking into on a plane ride or a gray winter
day. Sometimes I'll read and love a book but over time its images slip away;
those of *The Hive and the Honey* lodged fast and remain as vivid as those
in a dream."
—*VANITY FAIR*, Our 20 Favorite Books of 2023

"Paul Yoon masterfully explores the shared history, displacement, alienation,
and the lasting effects of war. . . . Yoon's lean and cutting prose dissects
truth and inheritance, interweaves haunting tales with mundane lives, and
reveals far-flung characters searching for home."
—*ELECTRIC LITERATURE*, Electric Lit's Best Short Story Collections of 2023

A NEW YORK TIMES EDITORS' CHOICE

Praise for THE HIVE AND THE HONEY

"Yoon tells the stories of characters at odds with their relationships to home and explores how trauma can linger in the most unexpected ways."

—*TIME*, The 10 Best Fiction Books of 2023

"In seven virtuosic stories centering characters that include a seventeenth-century samurai and a contemporary New York immigrant, Yoon captures scenes of the Korean diaspora."

—*Vanity Fair*, 13 New Books to Read This Month

"Yoon's new short story collection is another spare, controlled masterpiece, comprising seven exquisite stories highlighting the Korean diaspora scattered across time and oceans."

—Terry Hong, *Booklist* (starred review)

"Expansive, haunting, and intimate, Paul Yoon's new short story collection *The Hive and the Honey* shows Yoon at the height of his powers. Following characters of the Korean diaspora throughout history and across geographies, the collection's stories ask essential questions about how we build families and homes."

—Sabir Sultan, PEN America

"Yoon carefully mingles the extraordinary with the everyday, evoking the natural world with simple yet striking language. . . . This is an elegant exploration of life's brutal and beautiful moments."

—*Publishers Weekly*

"The third short story collection (his first since 2017's *The Mountain*) from Young Lions Fiction Award winner and Guggenheim Fellow Yoon spans cultures and centuries, roving from small-town New York, where a formerly incarcerated man tries to start a new life, to the Edo period in Japan, where a Samurai escorts an orphan boy back to his countrymen. Yoon's 2020 novel-in-stories, *Run Me to Earth*——a subtly devastating panoramic portrait of three lives displaced by war——was one of the standout books of that year, so I'm pretty damn excited for this one."

—*Literary Hub*, Lit Hub's Most Anticipated Books of 2023

"A complex look at alienation, identity, and the lasting effects of war . . . Yoon's attention to historic detail makes these tales of displaced people all the more affecting."

—*TIME*, The 36 Most Anticipated Books of Fall 2023

"Stories that echo with the loss, regret, and hope of migrants and nomads."

—*Kirkus Reviews*

"Yoon weaves complex tales of belonging and identity, of cultures clashing and building upon each other to create the multitudes that exist within communities."

—Patricia Thang, *Book Riot*

"The stories in *The Hive and the Honey* are geographically and temporally diverse. Each opens an inviting door to a seemingly calm moment in life, only to cast the readers into the deep and murky undercurrent of history. Amid violence are moments of gentleness; underneath darkness and bleakness are glimpses of light and humor. Yoon is a beautiful and beguiling writer, and should be called a national——or international——treasure!"

—Yiyun Li, author of *A Thousand Years of Good Prayers*

"*The Hive and the Honey* is much more than an exquisite, beautiful collection of short stories. Yoon roves geographic and historical points, catching stories of the Korean diaspora and, in the best way, the way of great literature, locates narratives that would disappear forever if he didn't find them, characters far from home, longing for home, finding ways to reconcile and embrace complex new landscapes. This is a book about all of us. If you let each of these wonderful stories into your soul, you'll feel the way I felt when I read this collection. I was in the hands of a vivid, powerfully honed imagination and came out better, more human, having learned something new about the world."

—David Means, author of *Two Nurses, Smoking*

THE HIVE
AND
THE HONEY

STORIES

PAUL YOON

MARYSUE
RUCCI
BOOKS

New York   London   Toronto   Sydney   New Delhi

**MARYSUE
RUCCI
BOOKS**

Marysue Rucci Books
An Imprint of Simon & Schuster, LLC
1230 Avenue of the Americas
New York, NY 10020

First Marysue Rucci Books trade paperback edition October 2024

MARYSUE RUCCI BOOKS and colophon are trademarks of Simon & Schuster, LLC

Simon & Schuster: Celebrating 100 Years of Publishing in 2024

For information about special discounts for bulk purchases, please contact
Simon & Schuster Special Sales at 1-866-506-1949 or business@simonandschuster.com.

The Simon & Schuster Speakers Bureau can bring authors to your live event.
For more information or to book an event, contact the Simon & Schuster Speakers Bureau at
1-866-248-3049 or visit our website at www.simonspeakers.com.

Interior design by Lexy East

Manufactured in the United States of America

1   3   5   7   9   10   8   6   4   2

Library of Congress Cataloging-in-Publication Data is available.

ISBN 978-1-6680-2079-1
ISBN 978-1-6680-2080-7 (pbk)
ISBN 978-1-6680-2081-4 (ebook)

For Don Lee,
for Michael Collier,
for Russell Perreault (1967–2019)

And to remember forever that
everything is possible when you stand
on the shore, looking out to sea.

—LUIS SAGASTI,
TRANSLATED BY FIONN PETCH

CONTENTS

BOSUN

1

KOMAROV

25

AT THE POST STATION

43

CROMER

69

THE HIVE AND THE HONEY

89

PERSON OF KOREA

105

VALLEY OF THE MOON

125

ACKNOWLEDGMENTS

149

BOSUN

During his twelve years in New York City, Bosun, who went by Bo, got into some bad business with an import-export company in Queens. It turned out the company was dealing in stolen goods, and Bo, who drove a truck for them, was eventually caught one winter on the bridge between Manhattan and New Jersey.

He would have very little memory of that moment other than the lights and falling snow. He would later be told that he leapt out of the truck and ran straight toward the bridge's railing. Perhaps he was disoriented by fear and didn't know where he was going. Perhaps in his disorientation and fear he thought of surviving a jump and swimming down the Hudson. In any case, a policeman tackled him before he could make it to the edge.

This was in the early 1990s. Bo lived alone in an apartment in a brick building in Jackson Heights. He took the bus every morning to the warehouse where he was assigned a truck and a schedule of deliveries to shops and restaurants all over the tri-state area. He got home before dark and what social life he had revolved around the kitchen staff of a nearby bar where he liked to play cards and where they gave him free food. He liked baseball—the Mets—and hot dogs, owned a single pair of work boots and a few days' worth of clothes that took up less than half of a closet. He washed his clothes once a week at the laundromat down the street where the old woman behind the counter happened to be from the same town where he had been born. Some days he helped out for a free wash, slipping a flathead into the crevices between machines and picking out dust and lint.

He was thirty-one years old.

He couldn't afford a good lawyer, but it wouldn't have mattered. They were all caught, everyone at the warehouse, then charged and sentenced quickly.

The drive up to the correctional facility was a wonder. He had never left the tri-state area before. He almost forgot where he was going. For six hours, through caged windows, he watched the land turn from a river valley to a vast flatness. Then mountains. They passed other smaller cities. Other rivers. Endless billboards for radio stations, cars, casinos, and good lawyers.

There was no one else from the warehouse on the bus, and in the ten months to come in that upstate facility, not far from the Canadian border, Bo would never run into anyone he recognized. For all he knew he was the only one. In a way that seemed both strange and not strange at all, he began to forget their faces—the faces of his boss and other drivers he crossed paths with every morning and evening. Then he forgot the faces of the card-playing kitchen staff and of the old woman at the laundromat.

In his cell at night he shut his eyes and tried to focus on the face of someone, anyone, but none came. It was as though he had always lived here in the prison. Even his dreams were of the place, most often of wandering its brightly lit corridors, dining hall, or library as if they were all his, as if the facility was only there for him. What startled him awake every time was that in the dream the weather came inside through the walls and roof—sudden rainfall, a flood, snow.

•

There were days when Bo convinced himself that his time in the correctional facility wasn't so bad. The food wasn't so bad. He liked the tater tots and potpies, and of course the hot dogs. He got to watch the Mets and run laps in the yard. He didn't have to worry about washing his clothes, missing the bus, or being too early or late for anything. He got used to all the lights, pretending he was at a ball game.

He got along with his cellmate. His name was Roger, who introduced himself as "part Mohawk, part nothing good." Roger laughed at his own joke; then they asked each other what they were in for.

Roger had gotten into some money misunderstandings, as he put it, in the nearby casino where he used to be a croupier. He admitted there were other things too but left it at that, waving his hand as though swatting away a fly.

Roger had the top bunk. He was tall and heavy, and every time he shifted the mattress sagged a little. The fabric was sand-colored. At night, Bo imagined he was looking down at an ever-shifting desert.

In the daytime, they took walks together in the yard. Roger introduced Bo to some of the other Mohawks and then to the Chinese and Vietnamese, who asked where he was from, saying that he didn't really look Korean. In the yard they said the Koreans in Queens were vicious, and they promised Bo they wouldn't mess with him because they knew he was vicious. Bo couldn't tell if they were joking. They exchanged stories about what they were in for; then they played soccer together, calling it the World Cup.

It was Roger who first asked if Bo played cards. The weather was getting colder and there was less to do. He had a few shiny decks and in the evening after dinner, in their cell, they played—mostly blackjack, because that was Roger's game and something Bo didn't know all that well. Roger was the dealer and advised Bo on when to hit, stay, or split, then flipped over his hole card.

They did this over and over and then switched roles. They played so much Bo could feel the sleek cards on his fingers even when he wasn't holding them, a ghostly set that always wanted to be played wherever he was during whatever he was assigned to be doing.

If he ever wanted to play, Roger said, when he got out, the casino was near a town called Calais. It had begun as an old French Canadian community, Roger said, whose members came down across the border and bought up land to farm. He said it was named after the real Calais in France. Bo pretended to know where that was.

Roger said it was like that everywhere here, small old towns with nothing in between. He said some town names out loud: "Westville, Moira, Fort Covington, Bombay," and Bo thought these strange.

Bo thought he would eventually miss Queens or perhaps even South Korea, where he had spent the first eighteen years of his life, but as the months went on, they were like the faces he tried to recall: far away, as though the places he'd once lived had been homes to someone else.

Roger asked him to referee the soccer matches. This terrified Bo. Almost everyone who played was larger and stronger than he was, and he would find himself shutting his eyes as he slipped between two bodies coming at each other, not realizing he was screaming. Sometimes this startled them enough to calm down on their own. Other times they fought Bo instead, and he would curl into a ball as quickly as he could, taking punches and kicks, covering his ears and searching for some hole in his mind to slip into as he waited for the whistle or a guard to rush over.

One day, in the middle of a game, he saw Roger in the small dirt yard, unmoving while other players ran up and down. Bo limped across. When Roger saw him, he began to shake.

6

"I can't be here anymore," he said, and buried his face against Bo's arm.

Roger didn't speak to him for a few days after that. Not in the cell or in the yard or at mealtimes. They ate with the others and lay down on their beds when they were supposed to sleep, but they didn't talk to each other.

From the bottom bunk, Bo watched the mattress shift. Maybe he had been wrong. Maybe it didn't look like the desert. It was as if he had discovered something, but it had slipped away. He tried to recall the last time he had felt a longing.

He avoided touching the wall and said the old town names to himself: "Westville, Bombay, Fort Covington, Calais."

He thought of French Canadians coming down over the Saint Lawrence, of ancient settlers meeting the Mohawk.

"You forgot Moira," Roger said in the dark.

Spring came, then Bo's last day. He said good-bye to Roger, who gave him a brand-new deck of cards. He said goodbye to his soccer teammates, who pretended they had never laid a hand on him. Led outside, past the walls, Bo walked down the driveway to a bus stop. He didn't feel like sitting. He looked up at the distant prison walls on the ridge and at a tree he'd never noticed from inside. A bus came. Visitors were dropped off. He watched them climb the hill.

Another bus arrived. It wasn't the one that would take him back down to the city. It was a local bus, the one Roger had told him to take, and Bo stepped in.

•

In Calais, he found a laundromat. Inside, on a corkboard on the wall, was an advertisement for a furnished house for rent. It was half of what he had paid a month in Jackson Heights. Behind the counter a man was chewing gum loudly and folding the wrapper into a neat square. Bo asked where the house was and the man looked at him hard, then pointed down a road: "Between here and the casino." Bo told him a flathead was good for picking lint out of the crevices of the machines and then he returned outside.

Calais was the smallest town, a street of three blocks and not much else. People looked at him from the sidewalk, from behind windows, in the sporting goods store where he bought packages of socks and underwear and a shirt, using up almost all his cash. He wondered if they stared because of his skin color or because it was somehow obvious he had been at the prison. Probably both. He kept touching his belt because he was unused to wearing one.

Bo walked for an hour. He followed fields and more fields. A greenhouse. He came to a hay farm with a long driveway that led up a slope, not unlike the prison, and saw an enormous house on the ridge with a porch. He almost walked by, realizing slowly that this was the address on the advertisement.

So he went up. He passed trees, distant hay bales, and a pickup, climbed the porch steps, and was answered by a dog barking when he knocked. He stepped back. Through a window, he could see a small couch and shelves filled with books. A rifle.

The door opened. An old man with bushy gray eyebrows was standing in front of him. Bo handed him the advertisement. The man held the ad close to his eyes and said, "I wasn't aware she did that," and handed it back to him.

Bo thought he was going to shut the door, but instead he reached for a vest on a coatrack and walked outside. The dog followed. It was a brown dog that seemed to know where they were going; it went on ahead, following a faint path in the sloping field, its grass slightly shorter, leading to a small cottage on the edge of the property.

The door was ajar. "The wind does that," the old man said. He pushed the door open some more, afternoon light arcing across the floor, and the three of them went in. The dog jumped onto a dusty couch by a fireplace.

There were only two rooms—a bedroom off to the side and a living space at the center that opened out to a kitchenette. There was the couch, a coffee table, and a small round wooden table with two chairs. A bookshelf and sun-faded landscape paintings that could have depicted here or Europe.

"You aren't a killer or a pedophile, right?"

"Right," Bo said.

"You Chinese? Mohawk?"

"Sure," Bo said, hesitating.

He took out the rest of his money. The man counted the bills and then looked at him again, his expression not unlike the man at the laundromat. Bo could hear his breath. Then Bo said that was all of it, everything he had, that he would need to look for work to get more, but he would do so right away. The dog rested its head over the back of the couch and watched.

"You like dogs?"

"Yes," Bo said, which was true. He'd had three growing up, what his mother used to call outside dogs. They kept guard, kept getting into the rat poison, one after the other, and suffocated, but he had loved them.

The old man spit on his shirtsleeve and wiped grime from the front window, then pointed at the bales. He said it was just him and his daughter here, and the migrants who baled the hay.

Bo knew nothing about hay.

"My name is Philippe," the man said. He was about to leave when Bo asked where the casino was. Philippe said to just keep going down the road. "You have a car?"

Bo shook his head.

"There's a bicycle," Philippe said. "Side of the house, near the kitchen entrance. Don't steal my food."

Philippe left, leaving the door ajar. Bo hadn't realized how hungry he was until the old man said the word *food*. He was also very thirsty. He turned on the kitchen tap. He let the water run for half a minute, staring at patterned tiles on the wall, then leaned over and drank. Bo kept drinking as the dog, still watching, made room for him on the couch.

•

Not everyone at the casino thought unkindly of Roger. The next morning, when Bo bicycled over, a man named Charlie met him on the floor and said, "Roger called yesterday. He said you're vicious."

Charlie looked him up and down and extended his hand. The handshake felt like a test, so Bo shook firmly, which Charlie seemed to approve of. He stood by Bo and together they scanned the main floor. The slot machines were on the right and the tables were on the left. It was morning, and more crowded than Bo expected it to be.

Charlie said they got busier during the summers because families came to hike the Adirondacks and then got bored of nature, so mostly the fathers slipped away and visited the casino. Bo nodded, still unsure whether he was going to get a job. Charlie was perhaps Bo's father's age, or around that, though Bo had forgotten how old his father was.

The hotel was stacked above, four stories tall, each level with a railing so you could look down and watch the games. Some people were doing that now as Charlie led him through the floor and oriented him. A waiter passed by, lifting a single highball with a red straw off his tray. Bo wasn't sure why, but it made him wonder what Roger was doing at this moment, whether he was reading or playing some solitaire. Then

he realized Roger would have another cellmate by now, and he wondered who that was.

Charlie took him downstairs, showed him the monitor room
with the CC televisions, the laundry room where a worker was
throwing large bundles of bedsheets into the washing machines, and
the lockers.

Charlie placed a foot on a wooden bench. He said Bo was to be
paired with Harry, and he could start right now if he wanted. That he
would be given a week's advance and from then on he would get paid
every two weeks. That it was going to be in cash, and Charlie hoped he
was all right with that.

Bo still didn't know what he was doing.

"Security," Charlie said, and selected a uniform off the rack.

•

Harry was a large man with tattoos all along his arms. He had finished
two tours in the Persian Gulf—"most uneventful and boring war I've
ever witnessed"—and come home to make a little money and "bust
some heads." He made a fist with his hand and punched the palm of the
other. He was a few years younger than Bo.

They put on their earpieces and staked out a corner of the floor
for half an hour, then moved to another. They watched the tables and
slots, and occasionally Harry pointed at a man or woman who seemed
suspicious to him for reasons Bo wasn't entirely sure about. They either followed, if the person was moving, or hovered, though nothing
ever happened.

Unlike the prison the casino was dimly lit, but like the prison
there were no windows. There were also no clocks, so Bo wasn't ever
sure what time it was. He thought he would get used to the sounds
of the slots and the perpetual hum of voices, but he hadn't yet. He

shifted his weight from one foot to the other. In the prison, if he was standing it meant he was moving. It was odd to stand but not move.

Bo looked up and spotted a child running fast along the third-floor balcony railing.

"Shit," Harry said, and hurried through a service door. Bo followed. He found Harry with the boy, who was around five, at the top of the stairwell. Harry was quietly but sternly chastising him and shaking him slightly. When Harry saw Bo, he said, "Meet my kid," and the kid tried to wave but Harry was still gripping him.

He learned that Harry was recently divorced but that he had custody of the child for a few weeks while his ex-wife was on vacation in Florida. He said *vacation* like it was his ex-wife's fault for going on one. He couldn't afford a sitter, so he had brought the boy here. He made Bo promise not to tell anyone. And then he sent his son back downstairs, where he was supposed to be hanging out with the laundry workers and kitchen staff. He shouted that the good ice cream was in the left freezer. His voice boomed in the stairwell.

As the child headed down, Harry sat on a step, punching his palm. He rubbed his face and breathed loudly. He had not told Bo the child's name. The boy had brown hair that was neatly combed, and he had been holding a paper airplane.

"He looks like a good kid," Bo said, not knowing what else to say. He was remembering how he used to get in trouble as a child because he liked to wander all over. He was always sneaking off into the alleys or to the GI base to spot the Americans. If he danced in front of them or sang an American song, they gave him a chocolate bar or chewing gum or, even better, some money. They stabbed his shoulders with their fingers to keep him dancing, sometimes causing him to fall, and they picked him back up and poked him again. He called those men the vilest things but with a grin, and they didn't understand his words. "You're a good kid," they always said before heading back into buildings where the lights were always on, flat as a wire on the horizon seen from Bo's house.

When he and Harry returned to the floor, a drunk man collided with a waiter, who then dropped his tray. The drunk began to curse and flail, and his elbow hit a woman who had been playing blackjack. She screamed. Harry ran over, grabbed the man by his jacket lapel, and brought him outside. Again, Bo followed.

The man continued to be loud and belligerent outside. Harry lifted him up and pushed him away as though he were a grocery cart, off toward a parking lot around the side. It was then that the man swung, hitting Harry on the side of his face.

It was a solid, hard punch that brought Harry to his knees. Bo thought Harry would get up immediately and strike back, and maybe he would have, but Bo stepped in. He was aware of what he was doing, yet it felt like a memory, like an action from the far past. He held the man's shirt collar, looked into his face, which was like a dried-up sponge, and kept hitting him. Then he switched hands. Bo felt the skin along his knuckles tear, he thought he even heard it, like fabric ripping.

When the man collapsed, Bo shouted once and hit the wall with both of his bloody fists, staining the concrete, and he felt Harry gripping him the way he had held his kid. Harry whispered into Bo's ear, but Bo didn't hear. He turned and began to pace and then, calming, stopped. Harry knelt to check on the drunk, who started to cry, saying that he had lost too much today, lost too much.

Harry wiped the blood off the man's face with a handkerchief. Most of it was from Bo's knuckles. Then Harry turned to Bo and examined his torn-up hands, almost tenderly, under the sun—it was not yet noon, cars sped down the main road, and the casino sign blinked high and tall.

•

Bo bicycled back to the hay farm in the late afternoon. It felt good to ride. He pedaled hard and let his feet go, letting momentum take him down the road. He stopped at a roadside shack to buy bottles of water and strawberries. He placed a carton of strawberries in a plastic bag hanging from the handlebars as he pedaled the rest of the way.

After the fight, Harry had brought him to the lockers and taped up his hands. He made a joke about the drunk's face being dense as a tree. Bo could hardly move his fingers. He wondered about broken bones but didn't say anything. He could still feel the throb of it now as he left the strawberries, along with what remained of his advance, by the front door of the main house.

He wanted to keep thinking of the bike ride, but that was gone. He thought about what had made him do such a thing, how quickly, and how he kept at it. He thought he wouldn't be invited back to the casino, but Charlie had been impressed by what Harry had told him—that they had found a winner "better than a soldier." By chance it had happened where there were no cameras and no witnesses had come forward, so it was just Harry's word.

"Bad men out and the good ones in," Charlie said, adding, "and keep those bandages on for as long as you can, they look great."

Bo was about to leave the porch when he spotted Philippe through a window, sitting by a fireplace with the dog beside him on the floor. There was no fire, too hot for that, but Philippe was listening to the radio, or what Bo thought was the radio until he looked farther in and saw a young woman, perhaps Bo's age, playing an upright piano.

The dog saw him through the window but didn't move. It was as if the dog were keeping Bo a secret. Bo stayed where he was, listening to the music come faintly through the window. The piano player had her back to him. He watched her hands. Or her fingers. They moved like a current of water. Above her was a framed photo of a person in a long coat and a child standing on the bank of a river where there was an island.

On the porch, the wind came up from behind, and he was suddenly very tired.

He left as quietly as he could and headed down the path to the guesthouse. Near and far and around him were giant hay bales. They seemed not to belong on earth—or they were from so long ago there was no place for them anymore.

A bird flew overhead.

The door was ajar. He went straight to the couch, resting his bandaged hands on his lap. He must have drifted off because when he opened his eyes again there was a person leaving the cabin, a silhouette caught briefly in the doorframe. She turned; she must have heard him. It was the piano player.

"I brought over some food," she said.

"What time is it?"

"It's six."

"In the evening?"

She laughed. "No. You've been out all afternoon and night. Just like yesterday. You sleep a lot. What are you, a boxer or something?"

She was referring to the bandages. He smiled. She said her name was Caro and that she could take a look at it if he wanted, but Bo refused.

She was still by the door. She wore old overalls and had a small mouth and a little darkness under her eyes. On the table was a plate of cold meats, cheese, bread, and some of the strawberries he had left on the porch, halved.

"That was a kind thing," she said. "The strawberries."

He broke off a heel of bread and folded some meat and cheese into it, then ate. "It's good, thank you," he said, and ate some more. "Do you have a phone I could use?"

He walked outside with her. It was cold. He wasn't expecting that. The dim sky had streaks of light and clouds. He tried to recall when he had seen such a big sky before. It almost made him stop. He breathed. It was cold enough that his breath was visible as it came out. He saw the dog trot over from the distance and bent down to pet it as it left a trail of dew across his jeans.

"He goes on adventures," Caro said. "And he won't ever tell me where."

Bo asked how long they had been here for.

"Me?" she said. "Off and on. My second life didn't work out so well, so I came back to my first."

She brought him into the kitchen using the side door. The phone was on the wall, with a long cord that could extend across the entire room, but he stayed nearby as he dialed and heard the rings.

He didn't recognize the voice of the guard who picked up, but he said it was Bo and asked whether it was possible to leave Roger a message.

"Who and who?" the guard said, and Bo repeated himself.

"Is this a joke?" the guard said, and hung up.

He kept the handset by his ear a moment longer, thinking of the yard and the library, then returned it to the cradle. Caro was pretending not to listen, wiping down a counter. She had put on an apron. She said her father liked his eggs scrambled because he was a bit scrambled. She spun her finger over the side of her head and then cracked some eggs into a bowl.

He felt like he shouldn't be looking around the room, so he kept his eyes outside, listening to the whisk swirling inside the bowl. He wanted to say he saw her playing the piano but wasn't sure how she would respond.

"There's a party tonight," she said. "At the hangar. Well, there's always a party at the hangar. But you can come if you want."

He didn't know what the hangar was. He thanked her and told her he had to work tonight.

"My money's on you," she said, and shook her fist at him.

•

Bo worked shifts all that week. He met Harry at the lockers and sneaked in some of his laundry to run loads the way the other workers did. Harry's boy ran around.

Each day they rotated stations every half an hour. The bartenders began to recognize Bo and slid him a Coke or a water. He and Harry looked for cheats, though oftentimes Bo ended up just watching the game. At the blackjack table, the players hit and stayed and split. Most times they lost, but sometimes, rarely, he watched somebody beat the dealer and a feeling came over him as he stood there behind the other players. He clapped softly and hurried to keep up with Harry.

They never spoke about the first day. His hands grew better, but they still hurt, faint but persistent, reminding him. He kept them taped up.

One day toward the end of the week, a paper airplane flew down from the fourth-floor balcony. It flew slowly and spun near them, so Bo caught it. Harry didn't see because Bo was walking behind. Bo folded it flat and tucked it into his jacket pocket. He didn't look up again.

Harry lived in an apartment building nearby. After their shift, he wanted to know if Bo would have a drink, watch some baseball.

"Another time," Bo said.

They were smoking outside against the wall where Bo had hit the man. Someone had painted over his bloodstains. Harry was carrying his child, who had fallen asleep on his shoulder. Harry swayed his hips a little and blew the smoke away from the boy's face, slipping in and out of the light of the parking lot lamps. He kept bobbing and swaying, keeping that rhythm up so the boy didn't wake as they headed to the car.

All that week Caro kept leaving food for Bo. He bicycled back to find a tray on the table, the meat half gone and the dog snoring on the couch. He had yet to open Roger's deck of cards. He watched the dog's hind leg flutter, watched the moon through the window and the old paintings on the walls. An immense quiet.

He placed his hand on the side of the dog's belly, feeling the rise and fall.

He dreamed of snow.

The phone in the main house rang. From across the field, he heard Philippe calling to him. He went up the slope, following the path in the dark, Philippe small in the doorframe. He wondered where Caro was. When he walked in, Philippe said not to steal his food and asked if Bo knew how to play the piano. A plate of unfinished scrambled eggs was in the sink.

He held the phone, thinking it must be Roger, that he must have tracked Bo down, but it wasn't. It was Harry.

His boy had vanished, Harry said. He was gone.

•

That night, Bo joined the search. Harry got some of his apartment neighbors to go looking, and the police were called. They all split up. Harry knew the boy couldn't have gone far because he had seen him only ten minutes before he noticed he was gone. Harry had been washing dishes.

They wandered the apartment halls and knocked on doors. Some walked down the main road with flashlights, and still others got into cars and drove around. Harry made Bo promise to go looking within the triangle of the hay farm, the casino, and the apartment building.

Bo borrowed a flashlight from Philippe, crossed the road, and entered the hayfields. He walked from one field to the next. He met a road he hadn't yet been on and kept in the high grass, making himself small when a police car drove by. When the road was empty, he crossed and kept walking. That immense quiet again. He passed a farm in the distance, came upon a stream, jumped over it, and entered another stretch of woods.

He had no idea where he was. He knew it was silly, but as he kept walking he grew afraid. He thought of Harry's boy. He tried to imagine where a boy would go in Calais. He was surrounded by the trees and, he knew, identical fields on all sides. An identical horizon, as though all directions were the same.

It was then that he heard music. It was faint, but he clung to it and followed, hurrying now through the woods until he came out on the other side, facing a chain-link fence. Beyond it was an airfield. Someone had slashed the fence, so he crawled through and hurried across the runway. Already he could see a crowd inside an open hangar, the dim light. It was like the mouth of an extinct creature, or one of those half-finished buildings in Manhattan that he could see from across the river. He paused at the edge, in a border of light.

The music was loud but pleasant. People drank from plastic cups and danced close together. He went up to the first group and asked if a boy about five years of age had come through, and they shook their heads. He moved to a couple kissing on a torn, stained velvet couch and interrupted them. He recognized some casino workers, the laundry crew and kitchen staff, out of their uniforms, wearing T-shirts and jeans. From somewhere farther in, glass shattered and a bird flew up toward the high rafters.

"How're the hands, Boxer?"

He turned to see Caro holding out the joint she was smoking. She was wearing a pale cotton dress that was maybe a little too big for her and her hair was up, revealing her neck. He took a drag of the joint and told her over the music that there was a boy missing. Harry's boy. Harry from casino security. That if he wasn't here, Bo should hurry and keep searching. He didn't realize he was talking very fast until she took one of his bandaged hands.

She asked if the police knew, and he said, "Yes."

Caro led him through the crowd to the back, where a young man sat on a beach chair, tapping his feet and listening to a police scanner. She said the young man made sure they didn't get found out. The DJ was asked to turn down the music, and they huddled together—the young man, the DJ, Caro, and Bo—listening to the scanner. The party-goers became curious and gathered around too.

They waited a long time in silence until a voice came on, saying the boy had been found. Someone in the crowd clapped. Then some more people joined in, and the DJ turned up the music and everyone started to dance.

"See?" Caro said. "Nothing to worry about. Who are they again?"

She tried to dance with him, but Bo didn't want to. He was still thinking of Harry and his son. His heart was beating fast. It was like she knew, could hear it too, because she stopped and said, "Let's go."

They took Caro's pickup to Harry's apartment building, where they found him and his boy sitting on the stoop out front. The child had been found by the shed where water and strawberries were sold, not far at all. He had wandered off, wanting to find his paper airplane. It turned out his mother had made it for him before she left for Florida.

Harry called himself a crummy father and cried.

Bo's chest went hollow and he blushed. He knew the paper airplane was in the guesthouse, in the pocket of his uniform, but he didn't tell them just yet. He listened as Caro mentioned to Harry that she had a son too, who lived with his father up north in Montreal. That she didn't see him often anymore. Eventually, Harry's boy fell asleep on Caro's lap, as if he had known her all his life.

"All that for a paper airplane," Harry said.

•

She didn't bring up her son again that night. It got very late. Late enough so that it seemed the events of the day had happened a lifetime ago. Caro thought maybe they had an hour left before it got bright. She walked Bo down the path toward the guesthouse, saying she liked this time best. They stopped midway, looking up at different corners of the sky.

"It was meant for a Canadian airline," Caro said. "The hangar. For airplane repairs. I remember when they were building it. I would bicycle over and watch it go up. It looked like the future. A spaceship or a city. But they lost funding, so no one owns it now. It's ours. You're using my bike, you know."

He said she could have the bike back if she wanted.

She laughed. She was a little stoned and drunk.

In the main house on the ridge, a light was on. A perfect square in the dark.

"He falls asleep by the fireplace," Caro said, still looking up. "I worry about him all the time. Is that healthy? I don't know. What's your full name?"

He hesitated, then told her.

"Like the officer on a ship?" she said, and he didn't know what she was talking about.

Caro explained that in English his name meant an officer on a ship who was responsible for the crew and equipment on board.

In his twelve years in New York and ten months in prison, Bo had never heard that.

She said she knew because her grandfather had been a bosun. There was a photo of him above the piano in their dining room. She said the funny thing was that her father's side of the family was from the other Calais, in France.

"The real one?" Bo said.

"Why is that one more real than this one?" Caro said.

He said he would like to go one day, just to see what it was like. She said it was a city by the water, and just then the field appeared aqueous to him. He could see its current. Wind and tide, as if they had found themselves suddenly far out at sea. Everything silver and hay bales like ships.

"My grandfather taught me this," Caro said, and lifted Bo's hands up, palms out, briefly tapping on the bandages. He kept his hands up as she stepped back off the path, raised her fists by her cheeks, and hopped a little on the balls of her feet. In the moonlight, she bounced, her skirt fluttering, and she lightly jabbed his left hand and his right. She asked if it hurt, and when he shook his head, she did it again, quickly and directly striking.

"Here," Caro said. "You try."

He didn't want to, but she approached and said it again.

"Left foot and shoulder angled at your opponent. Right foot at two o'clock. Back heels light, knees bent, right hand on cheek. You'll use that for the two. Think of it like a pulley system. One is the left, the jab, then two, the right. One, two. Step into it and step back. Eyes up."

He hit her hands. *One, two.* He stepped in and out and felt the grass skimming his ankles. He breathed and ignored the pain. The sound of his hits seemed to float out into the night. It was like an emptying. *One, two.* From somewhere distant, a car sped and faded. Caro looked at him and smiled. He did it one more time, then spotted the dog in a far field.

"There he is," Bo said.

"Going on a new adventure," Caro said. "Or the same old one."

As the dog headed farther away, Bo began to unwrap the bandages around his hands.

"Do you think I look vicious?" he said.

"Extraordinarily," Caro said, and circled him once, jabbing the air.

"Moira," he said. "Westville. Bombay. Fort Covington."

"What?"

Another wind came. He draped the bandages like a scarf over his neck and held on to the ends. He pictured Caro returning here, leaving her second life; her boy somewhere in Montreal. He thought of the old woman who ran the laundromat in Jackson Heights. He tried to remember her face again. The old woman had known those GIs on that base too. She used to ask, as he helped clean the laundry machines, how Bo's parents were. She never remembered his answer, or pretended not to, so that every time he had to say he had lost touch with them a long time ago, that they were probably somewhere in that town in South Korea that could feel small at times and vast at others.

Like this field, which was beside other fields.

Bo kept thinking of more questions he wanted to ask Caro. And as he stood there in the moonlight beside her, light on his heels, the air sweet-smelling, the wind, he suddenly felt that he had come a long way and that something great was going to happen to him, maybe not tonight or tomorrow, but soon. And he concentrated on it, wanting to make the feeling last as they talked through the last hour of the night.

KOMAROV

It was a small hill town on the Costa Brava. She arrived in the late afternoon, stepping off the crowded train that had come in from Barcelona, and followed the signs for the taxi stand. She was wearing the shirt she wore to work, because it was her nicest, and she was alone.

"Are you here for the fight?" the driver asked when she got in. "Not too violent for you?"

He winked at her through the rearview. Not knowing how to answer the first question—they hadn't talked about that—Jooyun hesitated. About the violence, she knew the driver meant because she was a woman and no longer young.

"Komarov," the driver said, and handed back a flyer. "You're here for Komarov, yes?"

She rolled down the window, not looking at him or the flyer, and said, "Yes," as he sped a little at a roundabout.

She didn't say anything else. The sun was everywhere. The ocean smell too.

She knew the room number, so when she entered the hotel she walked past the reception and took the elevator to the fifth floor. She found 512, paused to let a couple speaking in English continue down the sunlit hallway, and then knocked.

She could hear footsteps coming from inside the room. Then one of the young men she had met two days ago opened the door and let her in.

•

The year was 1980. A Friday in the first week of June. The doors to the small balcony were open and on occasion the white curtains billowed from the wind, briefly erasing the second man, who was sitting at the edge of the bed. The men had both loosened their neckties and were perspiring.

Jooyun kept still, fixed in some space between them, which was how she had felt since she had met them. In the bathroom, the faucet dripped. "It's been like that for days," the man behind her said in Korean. He squeezed past her and tried to tighten the handle anyway. The balcony curtains billowed again, and she fixed her gaze on the view outside: the flowers on the railing and, beyond that, the town covered in tiled rooftops that spilled down to the water. From the square came the sound of a woman singing.

"We wouldn't have blamed you," he said. "If you had changed your mind."

How could she have changed her mind? They knew she would have come regardless.

The one on the bed opened a bag. He explained to her that what was inside was a listening and recording device. That they were going to put a wire on her and that they would be somewhere nearby, discreetly listening and recording. He asked if that would be all right.

They hadn't told her that before. That was new. Jooyun quickly looked around. She nodded and stepped forward, placing the flyer at the foot of the bed, and unbuttoned her shirt in front of the two men, who began to work in silence; she could hear and feel their breathing.

They moved like a pair of enormous spiders around her, touching her as little as possible. As the mic slid up under a band and up between her breasts, she was aware that she was also sweating, that there was a smell coming from under her arms. She had spent all night smoking cigarettes and ironing her shirt, almost burning the back.

"Remember," one of them said. "You won't have long. Ten minutes. This is only the first of what we hope are many meetings."

"And remember," the other said. "At the end. Say something like, 'Perhaps we can keep talking,' and we'll wait for the response."

Jooyun kept nodding. On the side table near the balcony doors, next to the ashtray, she spotted a pen and a pad of paper. She asked the man behind her to light her a cigarette. Again, she heard the singing, and asked the men in the room if they had ever been to Spain before, and they said, "Keep talking."

They wanted to test the sound. Her mind went blank. She stepped toward the balcony doors, tapped the cigarette over the ashtray, and, waiting for a moment when they weren't looking, took the pen and slipped it into her pocket.

She then said something about how she had never been here, and about the glassware on the dresser—how it was proper to set them so that they didn't touch—and whether they could all hear the singing. Then she realized she wasn't saying any of this out loud.

She returned to the bed and picked up the flyer. The man closest to her looked over Jooyun's shoulder and said, first in Korean, then in Russian, that the heat here was making him boil and that, no, he had never been to Spain and that he was currently in the company of Lee Jooyun, fifty-four years old, born in North Korea, resident of Barcelona. And that the fighter on the left in the flyer was named Nikolay Komarov, a thirty-year-old middleweight boxer from the Soviet Union. Tomorrow would be his first match outside the Soviet Union, with an American, and Komarov had arrived last week with a trainer, a cutman, and at least two Russian bodyguards that they knew of. And that today, in an hour, before his sparring session, he would take a run along the Camí de Ronda on the coast with one of the bodyguards, who was their asset, and she would be there waiting for him.

He stopped. The other man, who had put on headphones and was fiddling with the machine, gave them a thumbs-up.

"Go out to the balcony," he said. "Let's test the wind."

What neither of them mentioned, but had told her two days ago, was that Nikolay Komarov was also her son.

•

She had been in Spain now for five years. Before that she worked in Hamburg, Germany, where she cleaned rooms at a hotel, which was what she did in Seoul before that. In Barcelona, Jooyun lived in a rooming house with other women from China, North Africa, and the Ukraine. They all cleaned houses and hotels and office buildings and museums. They came and went. They left bath products in the shared bathrooms for others to use and sometimes books or a video they could play on the television downstairs. Jooyun had been there the longest.

When Jooyun asked the Ukrainian about Komarov, the woman said she didn't follow that wretched sport. "But if you like large men, let me know," she said, and jumped into the shower as Jooyun got ready for her night shift, putting on her makeup before the bathroom mirror fogged.

That was yesterday. The day before, she had gone to the office like the other days, and afterward she had stepped out into the alley to find the two men already there by the dumpster, blocking the way to the street.

Her first thought when they began to speak was that someone had finally come to bring her back or to punish her for leaving. She had spent the war and after hearing about things like this. It didn't matter if you never went in and answered any questions the South might have for you—she never had—it didn't matter because you were a traitor. You had vanished once by running away, which gave them permission to erase you a second time—completely, wholly.

"Are you Lee Jooyun?"

They were very young with the same haircuts they would have gotten in Seoul. They also looked both tired and aware of everything. It was late but loud, the bars and the cafés in Las Ramblas all full and full of music.

Jooyun confirmed who she was and turned to throw the trash into the dumpster. She shut her eyes. In that moment, she believed it was possible that this would be her last breath, her arm in the air holding the trash and the shredded paper of a company whose purpose she had no idea about, her hands cracked from the bleach that seeped into her gloves, the bleach that had dimmed her sense of smell, the faint smell of the dumpster all over, the unending Barcelona night.

She opened her eyes.

Nothing happened. She heard the men share their last names, only their last names, Kye and Tak, and when she turned around, they were holding an open file folder. Inside was a picture of a man and a brief timeline of his life and hers. It was all there. The name of the North Korean village near the southern border that she had not seen or heard mention of in decades. The hotels she used to clean for. The Hamburg rooming house she had lived in and the current one. The child she had. The name of her husband who had gone on ahead, crossing the border the year before she escaped, and whom she never found.

The one named Kye pointed not at the line about her husband but above, at the child. Then he pointed at the photo in the file.

"This is him," Kye said. "The child you left behind. You left behind a child, yes?"

She had left behind a child. Yes.

They then told her who her son was—told her about the fight in the Costa Brava, and that it would be of great interest to them if they made contact with him.

She thought it was because he had been born in North Korea, but Tak said, "It would be beneficial for our country if we knew more about the Soviets."

"A relationship with our neighbor's neighbor," Kye added. "And so on and so forth."

"You want to see your son, yes?" Tak said.

"He wants to meet," Kye said. "He already knows about you. And he speaks Korean. The family that adopted him, the mother's side. She is a Korean from Kazakhstan, and she taught him."

Kye mentioned something about safety and that she shouldn't worry—by the time Jooyun arrived, it would all be arranged; they had someone on the inside.

The truth was that Jooyun had stopped listening to them. She was staring at the photo, unable to help herself: Did this young man look like her at all? Or her husband? She searched the face: what was clear was that he had broken his nose, maybe more than once. He had broad shoulders, a sharp chin, but his eyes were kind. Almost shy. She wondered if that made him a good fighter or not. Whether boxers cared about the eyes.

He had somehow gone farther north, probably smuggled across into Russia by a villager she once knew as well as she did the soil of that place and the weather forecast. She wondered how many in that village had survived. And how many of the children had survived.

Thirty years ago, 1950. She didn't have time to name her child.

She stayed in the alley and read more of the file. And then she tried pronouncing Nikolay Komarov, but couldn't, so she asked the men to help her, and they did as it grew later and louder in Las Ramblas.

•

The balcony wasn't large enough for two people, so Kye stayed in the room but close by. If the curtain blowing over him bothered him, she couldn't tell. Kye was trying to keep her talking. It was for testing the sound but also to keep her calm as they waited for the right time. The wire itched, but she ignored it.

Near the bay, a banner hanging between two streetlights was advertising the fight tomorrow at the stadium outside of town. Directly below was the sunlit square where vendors had set up stalls, selling food and souvenirs for tourists. There were people everywhere with their large hats and sunglasses and straw totes that held towels. She spotted the striped long-sleeved shirts and the cuffed shorts she knew were fashionable these days. Everyone appeared as though they had always been here.

Tak had given her water. She held the glass over the railing, scanning the shops, wondering if she should bring a gift to the meeting.

"Do you remember those years?"

Kye was asking her about her village. Home. She remembered the animals. The six dogs and the pigs and the goats. A loose floorboard where she hid the baby teeth that fell out of her mouth—were those still there? Then the drought and their hunger, their constant hunger until there were no more animals, and then more hunger. Also, a scar on her husband's wrist from an accident while chopping wood. The lightness of his body, lighter than hers. The sourness of his breath in the late night though she never minded.

"Did you use the valley route?" Kye said.

"What do you know of that?" Jooyun said.

"I forgot what it was called. The valley route."

She remembered. She remembered the girl who twisted her ankle and when she screamed the guide knocked her out with the butt of his rifle. They left her behind. Just like that. Jooyun's mouth going dry and her throat hollow as she kept walking with the rest. Moonlight on the stones and, between the stones, deep shadows.

She had a thousand questions for Kye and Tak, but every time she attempted to pluck one out, the questions slipped away. She felt like she was trying to catch kites whose strings she had lost.

Instead, she asked Kye why he did what he did. A sea breeze swept in, and the curtain swayed over him again.

"It's better these days," he said. "You should come back."

He was talking about Seoul. He said she would be inspired by the optimism all around. The hope and the hard work. The money pouring into schools. Education. Technology—he pointed back at the listening device—and medicine.

"In the war," Kye said. "You were assigned to a hospital, yes? You cleaned even then."

She glanced back at him. She took a sip of water and itched the side of her stomach.

There had been a field hospital near the settlement she had found herself in. She was assigned to mop the floors, boil the bedsheets. Forcing herself to look at every face in case it was her husband's. Then she would end her shift and go find a man, a living, breathing man—who cared who he was—which was how she obliterated herself during those years. Always men. She lost count. And not once another child growing inside of her.

She had left Korea the first chance she got. She had been gone for almost a decade now. With each year, she erased more of herself and grew older and more wrinkled and gray and cared less, only for two men to find her two days ago at the end of an alley halfway across the world.

She let go of the glass. She watched as it happened. It was like someone else had done it, like it wasn't her hand. She thought it would tip over the railing, but it fell on the balcony and shattered there. The noise snapped her away from wherever she was. She cursed and knelt. As Kye went to get the trash bin, the curtain billowing and hiding her, she took out the pen and quickly wrote on the flyer and then shoved the flyer into her pocket. Kye came back. Kneeling beside her, helping her collect the pieces of glass, he kept talking.

"I grew up next to a pharmacy," he said. "The pharmacist lived above the shop. Everyone knew who he really was, but no one talked about it. You see, he led people back and forth across. In those months right before the war. He brought families over. Or he brought a man back up north because the man had found a place for his family to live and wanted to bring them over. The pharmacist did this over a dozen times.

"Eventually, two young men and a young woman, all from the North, ended up staying with him. They survived the war. One of them, the woman, ended up a teacher at a school nearby. Another became a caretaker for the elderly, and cared for the pharmacist too when he grew old."

Kye stopped picking up the glass. Squatting against the railing, he wiped his brow and peered down at the square. Every time Jooyun looked at him, she was surprised at how young he appeared. How young were they when they started all this? How many were out there in the world doing what Kye and Tak were doing?

Kye went on: "One day the caretaker came like he always did. He cooked the pharmacist food. Turned on the radio. Settled him onto the couch with a blanket. Then he walked over to the bathroom and ran the bath. He undressed. He folded his clothes carefully on the floor, stepped into the water, and never came out.

"The teacher found him. She stopped by often too. You see, they all checked in on the pharmacist, even after all those years. That day the old man was still on the couch, awake, knowing something had happened but afraid to move. All night. His food untouched. His piss all over him. Afraid to move.

"You know what? That caretaker. The man in the tub. He used to leave me chocolate or a lollipop every time he stopped by. I was ten years old. That was my first. My first dead body."

Kye brought the trash bin back into the room. Jooyun checked her pocket.

"You said there were three," Jooyun said, when she joined them inside. "You said the pharmacist cared for three. What happened to the third?"

Kye shrugged. He didn't remember. "He wasn't part of the story," Kye said.

"Time," Tak said, interrupting them.

•

They left the hotel together. She and Kye. Tak was somewhere behind. She had promised not to turn and didn't. The summer heat was on the stones. With every step, she thought she was going to trip; without thinking, she slipped an arm around Kye. If this startled him, he didn't show it.

As they passed through the market square, and before Kye could tell her not to, she impulsively bought a T-shirt with *Costa Brava!* printed across the chest. She told the vendor to give her the largest size and to put it in a bag for her. She did all this quickly, handing him a bill, not staying for the change. Not once did she look at Kye, whose arm she kept holding. He was light as a shadow as they walked down toward the bay and found the start of the trail, which led up a cliff.

What seemed like the entire sea was visible from the top. The jagged coast and the other towns. Dozens of boats were on the water like tiny islands. Swimmers ran down the beach and climbed up on rocks and dove.

They found a long bench facing the water, and sat even though she didn't think she could sit still. Her heart was beating loudly and her gaze couldn't settle on anything. What time was it? She had no idea. Even after all these years she had yet to get used to the sun in Spain. "My heart," she said, and Kye told her to breathe and then wiped the sweat from his brow with a handkerchief. He said that they would both be nearby. He said again, "Ten minutes. That's all. The point is to see him again. Just ask, at the end. I'll be listening the whole time."

She didn't have time to acknowledge Kye. He left her and walked farther down the trail, and then a minute later, two joggers approached, slowed down, and she knew the one closest to the edge was him. What surprised her was that he wasn't as large as she thought he would be from the photo. Or perhaps it was the baggy tracksuit he was wearing. But she saw the broken nose and those eyes meeting hers. The bodyguard who had been jogging beside him let him approach alone.

Nikolay sat at the other end of the bench so that there was some space between them. He considered her and said in Korean, "Is it really you?"

When Jooyun stayed silent, her voice caught in her throat, Nikolay grinned and laughed a little.

"You're younger," he said. "Than how I think of you. You're younger."

She wondered if she was already disappointing him in some way.

In every way. She had thought about that last night, unable to sleep. Whether this man would be disappointed in her.

"Can he understand us?" Jooyun said. She was looking at the bodyguard who had moved toward the edge of the cliff. When Nikolay said, "No," Jooyun handed him the gift. He smiled again, thanking her, but didn't take the shirt out.

"You live here?" he said. "In Spain? That is what they tell me."

Jooyun told him about the office she cleaned. And about Hamburg and Seoul before that. He listened to everything, his eyes not leaving her, and then he said that he had gone all the way to Tashkent in the second year of his life to be adopted by a family. He had no memory of this. And now he was in Moscow because that was where there was good training and good fights.

Jooyun followed the movements of the bodyguard. "Tell me something about Tashkent," she said.

Nikolay thought about this. "There's a park. Near my parents' house. There used to be a small ancient stone there that said the path was part of the Silk Road. The trade route. Centuries and centuries ago. I used to like to go there and sit. My mother would give me Korean lessons and then I would go there. I don't know why, I'd think of the words or phrases I had trouble with. Then an earthquake hit the city when I was a teenager. It's a different place now. No evidence of the Silk Road. Gone. Poof. Who will remember it? Who will care? Did I care?"

He lifted his hands. They were thick as mallets. He seemed at ease and seemed happy to be talking to her. A couple walked by, pretending not to notice him.

"Do you know who got you out?" Jooyun said.

She meant who in the village. Nikolay didn't know. He said he ended up at a Russian church, which was where he spent the war years before moving west to Uzbekistan.

"Your parents," Jooyun said. "They're good to you?"

Nikolay nodded. "They run a restaurant. A Korean restaurant. I'm here for them."

It was then he explained to her that it was good money to fight here. To fight in Europe for the first time. It was a big deal for him not because of the fight, but because of the money.

"I'm here to put on a show," he said. "It's for the American. I'll lose. I'll get paid to lose. I can send the money to my parents."

She was surprised by his honesty.

"Sometimes," he said. "It's just business."

"And then the next?"

"The next fight I win," he said, and lifted his fists. He laughed again. He had a beautiful smile. A deep voice. She suddenly wished she knew the woman who had raised him. Had access to her. As though she lived down the hall at the rooming house so that Jooyun could knock on her door and lie in the bed together and talk to her.

She asked Nikolay what else he remembered about his early years, but he didn't know much. She looked down at the gift bag between them and told him she remembered the animals. And a woman who used to sing for them in the evenings. That she thought she'd heard her voice today and was wondering if she was going crazy. The woman had made it out, she told Nikolay. She lived in New York, outside the city, or at least she used to. There had been a time when they corresponded every year, but they hadn't done so in a long while. Jooyun thought that would get him to talk a bit, but he was now looking out at the water and the sun beginning its descent. He kept making fists with his hands.

The bodyguard circled in front of them and lifted two fingers. Two minutes.

Her heart began to beat loudly again. She could feel the wire sliding against her sweat. She asked what it was like to fight.

"You don't travel very far," he said. "Inside a ring. That's what I like about it."

"Do you care about the eyes?"

"The eyes?"

"When you box. Do you care about the opponent's eyes?"

"Collarbone," Nikolay said, and stood up. He went back to the path and shadowboxed a little to show her. She watched the power of him. The self-control and the centeredness of him. She had once watched a painter in Las Ramblas painting the image of an intricate cathedral. It was like that.

"Collarbones and shoulders," Nikolay said. "It's all there." He sat back down. He sighed and looked up at the long branches of a tree.

"Is anything coming to you?" Jooyun said.

Jooyun didn't know how else to say it. She had spent the last two days and the past nine minutes wondering if all this time she had been wrong, wondering if she had made a mistake, whether some kind of deeper, truer recognition would come to her as she sat beside this young man.

A bird flew over them and headed out to sea. She explained to Nikolay that she had gone across the border because she'd promised her husband she would. But that she never found him. And that she didn't know to this day whether her husband had survived, whether he was happy and healthy, whether he lived in Seoul or Spain or Tashkent or somewhere else, somewhere close or far, with another family or alone—whether he thought of her at all, the way she thought of him constantly, like an ocean tide, more than she thought of the son she'd left behind.

She asked if that was a horrible thing to say.

"Time," the bodyguard said in Russian, and tapped Nikolay on the knee and went down a bit on the path.

She searched Nikolay's face as he stood up again. He almost reached for her hand. He thanked her for the gift, the bag swaying around his finger, and as he turned to join his bodyguard, she tried to imagine their next meeting. And the one after. The long fantasy of this. The part she was playing, and perhaps the part he was playing too. The wanting. All those years of wanting.

What happened when her usefulness to these people who had brought her here ended?

She never said what she had been instructed to say.

They were about to head down the cliff when Jooyun stood from the bench and shouted his name.

Nikolay!

They both turned, the bodyguard suddenly alert.

Jooyun took a few steps toward them, pressing one hand against her chest, muffling the wire, and said, "In the village. The singer I told you about. She had a child. So did another. A basket weaver. Both children were born in the same year as mine. Six months apart, maybe less. All three were boys. All three."

What she refused to say next, the way she had refused to ask for more proof from Kye and Tak than a sheet of paper, was that her own son had died five hours after he was born. That Jooyun had held him and watched him die and then watched him for a while longer after he was dead. He never opened his eyes. She never shut hers. Sometime that night, she felt someone take her boy away and, as families were being separated in the chaos and the madness, someone else lifted her and carried her and that was how she left. She was carried away.

Jooyun let go of the wire. She could see the paths his mind leapt toward, the way he looked down at the bag he was holding, for the first time catching sight of the flyer she had slipped in there in the folds of the T-shirt, the name of the singer and the name of a New York town scribbled on the back. She never knew what had happened to the basket weaver, whether that woman had also made it out.

She wanted to tell Nikolay that the singer was a start. A start if he truly wanted to try.

He was still looking down at the bag, his expression unchanged. "Come to the fight," he said, his voice suddenly soft, shy, like a child's. "Come to the fight. I'll see you again."

And then before she could respond, he and his bodyguard were gone, and Kye was hurrying up from behind her.

"What did you say?" he said, taking her arm. "You said something. I know you did. What was it you said? It doesn't matter. You forgot to ask him, but it doesn't matter. He said it himself, didn't he? He did."

She began to walk away from him. "Please stop talking," she said. "Please leave me alone."

"We'll go to the fight," Kye said, ignoring her. "Yes. You were wonderful. I had a feeling about you. You were great. You'll see him again."

Jooyun screamed.

She covered her ears, stepped to the edge of the cliff, and screamed. The sound echoed down to the bay below where people shaded their eyes and watched a young man helping a woman back to the bench. When nothing else happened, the same people returned to watching the sunset. And the boats. And the last swimmers who climbed up onto a rock and dove, one after another, into the sunset's reflection.

AT THE POST STATION

Edo Period, 1608

1.

On the Tokaido, on the last day of our journey, we come upon a tree
that has flowered early. It stands alone amid the endless row of cedars
that line the road, its bright red color so sudden and distracting—
like the appearance of a door among the evergreens—that we fail to
notice at first the corpse not too far away, lying in a ditch.

Almost at once, Hiroko dismounts. He takes his sword from his
scabbard, but I signal to him. I look at my horse's ears and listen. When
the silence continues, I dismount as well and approach the ditch, inch-
ing my way down the slope, some of the red petals falling over us as
Hiroko follows.

It is, or was, a man. Someone, or more than one person, attempted to wrap the body in straw mats, though they did a poor job
of it. The wind or the animals or both have shifted the mats enough
to reveal the wounds that were inflicted upon him: his stomach has
been sliced open by a long blade, like ours, and the right shoulder
has been halved so that the head and the throat are almost completely
severed from the collarbone. His blood has long ago seeped into his
clothes and the earth around him. By my guess he has been dead for

two weeks, maybe more, and his eyes are open, but slightly cloudy, like tea.

What intrigues me is that he is a European. A Spaniard, perhaps. I say this because in my time I have met only Spaniards dressed the way he is—the missionaries who once a year or so visit the castles in our province. Though of course I cannot be certain of any of this. Nor can I be certain of the path to his death, whether it was incited by the man's religion or, simply, as it happens too often on this road, by words exchanged between two passing parties—an insult thrown, a gesture that carried disrespect. Just last year, when my lord and his retainers were traveling on this road to Edo for our yearly residency at the shogun's castle, we witnessed a small skirmish between two other daimyos and their respective retainers that caused the death of a young man. It turned out one lord had ordered the other's retainers to take off their hats and bow, and he was refused.

They carried the young man away, at least, and cleared the road as quickly as possible for us. I never saw any of them again. I am trying to recall if I ever learned who that young man was when Hiroko touches my wrist. I turn to peer up over the ditch. Standing on the side of the road, studying us and the scene before us, is the Korean boy we have been placed in charge of and have been escorting this past week along the Tokaido. I am ashamed to say that for a moment, or for several moments, I had completely forgotten about him. He is around ten years old, we believe, and he has no name. Or no name that I am aware of. He was in the care of my lord's son, but my lord's son died this past winter of disease, and now the boy is an orphan again.

Hiroko calls him a casualty of the invasion of Korea, where we took him, ten years ago, when he was an infant. In the chaos, I had been unsure what else to do with him, my arms listening to the command of my lord's son before fully understanding and coming to the awareness that I was lifting the boy toward him and his horse.

We call the boy Yumi, or *bow*, because of his talent with archery and because he is swift and near silent. When he speaks, it is quietly, and only in Japanese, which he has learned these past years. I have no idea what kind of life he has had with us, not truly, having to deal every day with the antics of my lord's son, who treated him like a circus animal and who was war-hungry and vain and lustful and gluttonous and most of all afraid of everything. I can't imagine a life under a man like him, but the boy is healthy and for the most part in good spirits, his eyes always alert and bright; and on most days, when I have the privilege of keeping him company in the practice hall for his archery lessons, I see no fear in him.

Like now. The way he stands up there at the edge of the ditch, almost glowing like a forest spirit, his excitement and curiosity about the body covered in straw mats growing in his eyes.

"You should stay up there," I say to the boy.

He doesn't listen, of course. He has hung his child's bow across his shoulder—he wouldn't leave without it, the arrows packed somewhere on the back of my horse. He tugs on the string slightly as his mind decides how best to proceed, choosing to sit and slide his butt down the slope. He slides faster than he predicted, and I catch him before his feet can disturb the corpse. He grins at me. If the smell of decay bothers him, he doesn't show it.

I take out a handkerchief I carry with me under my kimono and offer it to him. He places it over his nose and his mouth and proceeds to study the wounds as Hiroko begins to point, his finger hovering over the intestines and then the European's unkempt beard. To Hiroko's delight, there is a line of ants crawling up to the parted lips and vanishing inside the cave of the mouth to, I presume, lay their eggs.

"I passed through an old battlefield once," Hiroko tells the boy, not me, because I already know this story, I was there. "I went to pay my respects to the *bushi* who had died there, yes? And it was there that I saw for the first time a skeleton in a clearing, still wearing the armor the man had died in. And Yumi-san, guess what? A tree was growing out of the skeleton's mouth. A young cherry tree. Isn't that miraculous? We have this life, and then we become something else. Wouldn't you agree? You have had this life but soon, tomorrow, you will become someone else, with someone else. You mustn't be afraid of change like that. You must embrace it and be stronger for it. Just as the spirit of this man is now flourishing under shade, under the colors of these new blossoms, the branches protecting him from rain and snow."

"Hiroko," I say.

I mean to end this; we have been here too long, the boy doesn't need to hear about such things or see what he has seen. Then again, I also believe if the boy is interested, then he is interested. I cannot remember if he has ever laid eyes on a European before. In my recollection, he has seen only one other corpse in the past ten years, when I accompanied him to a game he was to participate in in another lord's court with other children who excelled at the martial arts. There was a family carrying someone in the back of a wheelbarrow, covered in an old banner, unaware that an arm had slipped out and the knuckles were dragging over the dirt road. I dismounted to assist them, Yumi still on the horse and watching in the same way he has been doing here, studying with Hiroko the ants in the mouth while also respecting the body by keeping his distance.

Perhaps our journey is proving to be educational in ways I have not foreseen. Hiroko is correct: at this time tomorrow, we will part ways with him and more than likely we will never see the boy again. I think it is better this way. He is finally free of my lord's son, and he is old enough to leave the confines of our care. He will begin again a life, a far more decent one, a more meaningful one.

Hiroko stops talking, bows slightly at me, though I know I have annoyed him by telling him to stop. I tell the boy to head back up and to check on the horses.

"Do we take him with us?" Hiroko says as the boy climbs, the soil now all over his traveling pants. Hiroko means the corpse.

"Let it be," I say.

Hiroko says, "Why are they so dirty? The Europeans. Look at that beard. The teeth and the fingernails. They dishonor themselves."

I tell Hiroko the man's cleanliness, or lack thereof, is the least of his problems. We exchange quick theories on what happened, conclude it was the religion—truth be told, because it seems the more dramatic story to us—and then in his smile I know Hiroko has forgiven me for interrupting his story.

By the time we return to the Tokaido road, the boy is holding the reins of both our horses, ready to go. He has quietly rooted through his belongings, found his arrows, and is now carrying them on his back, along with his bow. Clever boy.

A wind blows through the corridor the trees make, the red flowers that still look like a door to me trembling and falling against the cedars as we continue toward our destination.

2.

My name is Toshio Yamashita and I am twenty-nine years old and in service to my lord. We are from the eastern edge of the Mikawa province and have been traveling now for a week on the Tokaido, having entered the Musashi province, averaging about twelve *ri* per day, sometimes more, depending on the tiredness of the boy.

It is before the official start of spring, which was intentional on our part, in the hopes that we would not cross paths with many travelers or processions and their daimyos. I am still wearing my winter kimono because it is cold in the evenings, even at the post stations that swing toward the extravagant—in themselves like palaces—as well as others that have suffered from the years of war on this island and from the competition of other stations that have benefited from those wars.

I am told and reminded repeatedly that we have entered a period of peacetime. It seems true enough. We have become, as Hiroko says, errand boys, administrators, politicians, babysitters, guardians to a Korean orphan. I think Hiroko exaggerates. I have not minded these years. I have pushed that other part of me into a far corner and I do not often miss that person. My last battle was in Korea, where I lost a thumb and Hiroko a bit of his cheek that has turned into a pale scar. Sometimes in the evenings, when we have drunk too much, we like to imagine they have found each other on that dreaded peninsula, my thumb and his cheek, and they are living a good life together. Have they found their own tree to flourish in? Sometimes we are convinced the boy carries them near his heart, and that he will crush them one day, and we will feel the pain of that forever.

I act sometimes as though the boy Yumi scares me. I assure you, he does not. I have grown to like myself better these past years. To try to be more open about what passes through my head. Is that a silly thing for a warrior to say?

Hiroko, on the other hand, seems to grow more restless as the seasons pass. He spends more and more time at the brothel outside our castle, has had every disease that has not killed him, no longer exercises much, and believes his face wound gives him the right to stare boldly at anyone, both women and men alike, whatever suits his whimsy on that particular day. He can be wretched the way my lord's son was wretched—and I confess they were often wretched together—but Hiroko is the one I have known the longest, and I still see the humor and the kindness he had when we were younger as well as the strength that makes him the best of warriors. (I am also convinced he could still beat me in a duel, though I would never confess this to him!)

He is good to Yumi, even if he is at times, like when he was crouching beside that corpse, crass. Take for example what happened a few hours later on the road, when we found the river we would have to cross before reaching our destination. The melting snow had raised the water level so that it was almost touching the old wooden bridge, forceful enough to push it a bit side to side. Even so, because we had crossed the bridge so many times before on our way to Edo, we didn't think too much of it.

Or perhaps we were a bit tired, in denial of our tiredness, eager to reach the post station, eager for this mission to be done with, and therefore we hurried a little. The horses crossed the river easily. They had done this countless times before and knew the way. They climbed the bank, shook off the water, and began to graze, bored, waiting for us.

So we started over the footbridge, the boy between us. I wasn't always looking at where we were stepping, still in the wake of that corpse, perhaps, or something else that had not yet come to my mind's surface. Perhaps I was looking at the horses, admiring their ease and their stoicism. The water was loud enough so that I did not hear the crack and the break as the boy plummeted through a hole in the bridge. The truth is if it weren't for the arrows he was carrying on his back, we would have lost him completely. The arrows stopped his fall, and he hung there, dangling in the water, which sped over him just enough so that he was completely submerged but visible, his face looking up at the two of us as he began to drown.

Could we have acted quicker? I do not know how to answer this. I know something passed between Hiroko and me, the way it used to when we were in battle—a moment I cannot put into words—but it went away and we both reached down, lifted him back up, and hurried across. I tore away the boy's shirt, found a pulse, turned him to his side, and hit his back repeatedly until he woke, coughing, spitting out the river water. Hiroko laughed and slapped his thighs so loud the noise startled the horses.

Then the boy, aware of what had just happened, began to scream. He knelt toward me and swung twice, with both fists, barely hitting my chest, and screamed.

"Yumi-san," I said. "I'm sorry."

I kept saying that and held the boy's wrists until he calmed, and then I examined him until he told me sharply to stop fussing over him. I do not believe he has ever said this to me before. The confidence and the maturity of it startled me. So did, I confess, the strength of him as he struggled against my grasp. I told him again that I was sorry, that I should have been paying closer attention to the footing, and then Hiroko went for the boy's bag to find his spare clothes.

"Take mine instead," I said to Hiroko.

He hesitated. He bowed and passed me my bag, where there was a spare kimono. I laid it out on the grass, took out my short blade, and proceeded to trim the hem and cut the sleeves to match the length of the boy's arms.

It was a poor replacement, of course. He resembled the circus act my lord's son always desired him to be. But it greatly pleased the boy, wearing my kimono, which swallowed him, but as soon as we made our way toward the post station, he forgot about the incident at the river, or at least seemed to.

Hiroko, riding beside me, whispered that he didn't understand why I had done that to my kimono. I knew that his implication was that it was disrespectful to our uniforms, and therefore to ourselves and to our service, but I ignored him and placed pressure on the sides of my horse, riding ahead, the boy's arms around me as we approached the gate of the post station.

I felt no need to explain that if we had used the boy's spare clothes, he would have no more clothes left, and neither I nor Hiroko knew how much farther, and for how long, and where exactly the boy was going after tomorrow.

3.

Here are our orders: we are to wait at this designated post station for the arrival of a Korean who is a member of a tribute mission that has been touring Japan. We will transfer guardianship over to him, and then Yumi, we assume, will join the mission and eventually sail back to Korea, back to his country of origin, where he will be placed with a family and in a home.

The Koreans learned of the boy through my lord's son's wife, who has begun her residency in Edo this past year after her husband's death, as a gesture of good faith to the emperor. I have often wondered if an outsider would find these residencies odd. We have been doing this for decades. Many children and spouses of lords are there in the city for a set amount of time, participating in life under the gracious wing of the emperor. The lords and their retainers visit every other year. We buried her husband and afterward we brought her on this route, which was the last time I saw her.

Her name is Kakue and we grew up together. Though I dare not address her by her name in public anymore. When my lord brought up his intentions for the orphan boy, I thought at first we were heading all the way to Edo, and it well pleased me to think that I would see Kakue again. But it was not to be. There has been no way for us to communicate without inciting a scandal, and so I'm left wondering if she has adjusted to the city life, whether she remains in mourning, whether she truly ever was.

I do not understand what she ever saw in that man, but I understand the marriage was an opportune one in many other ways. I confess that if I had had a child close in age to marriage, I would be remiss if I ever pretended to be uncertain over which was the clear choice for a secure, lasting future: a lord or a samurai. I neither begrudge the life she chose nor do I begrudge mine. It is a great privilege to have spent my time in my lord's service with her nearby, inside the same castle walls, to spot her so often walking down a long hallway toward me in deep discussion with a visitor or a tutor and feel the joy it always brings me to step aside for her and bow.

In any case, thinking of this now makes me wonder what lies in store for the boy Yumi in the coming years. Whom he will meet. What his Korean name will be. Whether love, in the way I believe I understand love, will be involved in his eventual marriage, or whether marriage will be driven by something else.

I look at him now in the room we have reserved at the inn, his hair damp from his fall, and I try to picture him older, as old as I am now. I wonder what kind of man he will be and what kind of code he will follow.

I wonder whether we will meet again and whether that will be in battle.

A heat flares inside my chest. I scratch at it. Hiroko is lying on his mat, looking upside down at the window, wanting to visit the brothel, but pretending he doesn't want to.

The Korean was supposed to be here by the time we arrived, and it occurred to us that we may be at the wrong inn. There are by my guess twenty-five buildings in the station, and at least three are inns. Entering through the gate, we saw the front buildings with their tile roofs gleaming in the sun, and I was quite satisfied by the condition of this particular station and its cleanliness.

I was also, admittedly, relieved that there were no signs indicating a lord and his retainers were staying here—no wooden placards, no flags or sand piles in front of doors. (As I said, we have no desire to attract attention to ourselves.) But then, as we headed farther in, the buildings changed: tiles became thatch and then simple wooden boards warped by the weather and coated in mold. I have not visited this station in a long time; it's clear the years have taken their toll on it.

After placing our horses in their stalls, we asked the innkeeper if we could bathe in the hot spring, and he bowed deeply, apologizing, and said that a boulder had dislodged from the cliff's face, and that the spring would not be available until tomorrow afternoon. I said that was most unfortunate, that we had had an accident at the river, but the only thing the innkeeper could offer us with his sincerest apologies was buckets of hot water to bring to our room. I expected Hiroko to make a fuss—in fact, in another time I believe he would have challenged the man simply for his demeanor, or because he didn't bow deeply enough—but to my surprise, Hiroko shrugged and said, "No boulder fell over there, right?" He was pointing at the brothel.

"Indeed not," the innkeeper said, avoiding eye contact with us.

To add to his apology, the man brought over some cold sake that Hiroko has already depleted as I continue to wonder where the Korean is. I scratch at my chest. The boy, like Hiroko, but of course sober, is falling asleep on his mat, my cut-up kimono loose about him, some dried mud I missed staining his ankle like a birthmark.

"Should we have brought him with us?" he says, halfway in a dream. I think he is talking about the corpse, but then I wonder if he isn't. "My arrows," he continues, and says nothing else. The things that saved his life have bent so much they are now useless.

I tell Hiroko to keep an eye on the boy, that I will see if I can figure out what is causing the delay. He responds by lifting his short blade and twirling it in the air.

I step out. The afternoon has grown finer. There is a chill in the air; a narrow view of Mount Fuji lies in the far distance, beyond a cluster of hills, with snow covering its peak. I focus on this rather than the decrepit buildings around me, badly in need of renovation. In some ways, I suppose, I would rather be here than in a fine station, which would be far busier, with more crowds of people or other lords spotting the Korean boy or the Korean man we are waiting for, sparking their curiosity or their discrimination.

I wonder what it is like to be here on a tribute mission, meeting scholars and artists in the cities, what they really feel about each other, what motives truly lie in these visits and their days. I wonder if they are fueled by derision or hate, and I wonder if ten years is long enough to forget a war. Perhaps war has nothing to do with this at all. Perhaps we will always just distrust each other.

I think of the boy again under the water, looking up at us, his eyes empty to me, and then I stop an old man with a dog and ask if by chance he has heard of any visitors from Edo coming this way.

"Not yet," the old man says. "Haven't you heard? The river closest to the city. It overflowed. They have to wait for the level to go down before they can cross. I bet by tomorrow."

I thank the old man and watch as he leads the dog up past the temple to a row of stalls where vendors have set up their shops. It is a beautiful dog. A hunting dog. Then I recall that this area is known for breeding hunting dogs and that the station used to have a stall for the breeders.

I also recall that Yumi kept wanting a dog, though my lord's son never got him one. "You're the dog, my boy," he would always say, and pet him, and then pat him on his rump and tell him to fire another arrow at the apple on the table. Which the boy always struck, dead center, the noise and the shudder of the fruit causing even myself to stand up a bit straighter with pride.

Where does this talent come from? I have taught him what I could, but he is better than twelve archers in the heat of battle. Will this please whoever is to take care of him now or disgust them? Was he in another life a warrior and I his victim?

The stall with the dogs is still here. I am relieved that even in the station's condition, the breeders continue to come and that it seems people are buying the animals, as I see a man doing now, engaging in conversation with the one I spoke to earlier as he peers into the cages at the pups as well as at the older ones who lie or sit obediently beside the breeder.

In the next stall over, I find for sale a pile of scrolls and umbrellas, rows of portable chairs and wooden buckets one could use to carry water, sake, and soy sauce. In another, I find brushes, lanterns, and kelp. If I had come with my lord, he would purchase many of these things at all the stations, eventually giving them away as gifts in the city or to those waiting back home for him.

I browse the stalls the way he would, walking up the slight hill and back down. More people staying at the inns come up, most of them simply browsing and heading to the temple. I think I see the post station official in his uniform down below, ordering a pair of men to keep sweeping.

I am looking for extra clothes for a child, but there are only pairs of *geta* dangling from a string, their wooden soles clapping like chimes in the wind. I cannot help but study the selection of hand guards for swords—unimpressive—and it is there that I come upon arrows hanging on the wall. They are longer than the ones we made for the boy, these meant for an adult, but I purchase six anyway.

The seller smiles approvingly. "Six opportunities to find peace," he says to me, and bows.

I bow back. I am passing the stalls with the hunting dogs when one steps forward, thinking perhaps I am a potential owner. I rub the animal's soft ears, pause in the deepness of her eyes, then I bow to the old man, and keep walking.

At the inn, I explain to Hiroko about the river, that the Korean is delayed, and I tell him to prepare for a longer wait. As he reaches for the empty sake bottle, I relieve him so that he can stagger off to the brothel. It is almost evening, the boy fast asleep. I place the arrows beside his child bow, and I boil stickwort I found in the forest, glad Hiroko isn't here to tease me about how I have grown a taste for it, this plant we ate during wartime to survive. I have also brought with me a box of pickled eggplants and melons the court's chef hid away for us, and I snack on them, saving the last few for the boy when he wakes. The food, the hot drink, the boy's breathing bring on the tiredness of the journey and the excitement of today.

By now, the boy's hair has dried. His face contorts, as if he is in pain, and I almost wake him, but I don't. I watch the rapid movements of his eyes under his eyelids. Is he dreaming of being underwater again? Did he witness our hesitation and whatever passed between Hiroko and me?

Or is he dreaming of his home? His mother? Would an infant remember her? Would it be the smell of her or her heartbeat? I have not once asked what he thinks of all this. Not just of this week on the road and the lord's decision, but of everything. All these years. This life that was given to him because we took his first one before it even started. He has followed me obediently because he always has.

My mat is close enough to his so that I can reach out and touch his ankle where the dried mud is, and I do reach out. I hold him there, wondering if I will remember in the years to come what his ankle feels like, and what else of him I will remember. I can hear steps outside, the wooden clap of *geta*. Horses. A conversation about whether the river is passable. Talk of a festival in the city, the coming spring, doubts about whether this post station will last another year, a rumor that a better one is being built in this province.

My eyes grow heavy, and I am met with a memory of Kakue reaching up to pet a dog that had appeared while we were lying in a field, laughing and hiding from our families—the dog's excited snout all over us, his tail like a flag, his paws spread out, like two leaves, on Kakue's chest.

4.

The following morning, I wake alone. Hiroko's mat remains rolled up against the wall. The boy's is laid out flat beside mine. His bow, the new arrows, and his bag are gone. The room smells of us and the stickwort. I splash some stale water on my face and under my arms and dress quickly, grabbing my swords.

The sunlight is everywhere. I can spot the cloud of my breath. The station paths are damp from the night. I glance across at the passersby, but I cannot find the boy. I scan the hill, trying to think like him. I wonder what I might do. I realize I might go back to the river. Perhaps not because of the fall but because of the corpse farther on.

A few years ago, he used to run away all the time. We would have to go chasing after him. Once I found him in the cave of a gutter outside the city walls, balled up, screaming the way he did yesterday on the riverbank as I attempted to reach for him. So I sat across from him and waited and spoke to him for hours until he fell asleep, though I no longer remember what I said, only that I carried him back, thinking with every step that I didn't have to bring him back at all, and why was I doing so, the thought never going further than that.

I am hurrying to the horse stalls when I stop. In my periphery, I spot two men wearing straw hats in the garden of a teahouse, sitting on a wooden platform where a tray has been brought to them. Yumi sits across from them, his bow, the arrows, and his bag by his lap.

I enter from the back, my eyes never leaving the two men. They are dressed in new kimonos, and by the way the older one tugs at his sleeves I know they are not from anywhere near here. The garden is quiet. I grip the handle of my sword as I step down the stone path past the small shrine and the caged birds until the boy catches my presence and runs over.

"Toshio-san! You got me arrows!"

He is still wearing my cut-up kimono. He takes my hand and leads me to the two men. It is the loudest I have heard the boy speak in ages.

"Toshio-san," the boy goes on. "These men. They say they are here to take me back to the country where I am from. That I am not speaking my true language and that I will learn everything all over again. Is that true?"

I am in shock at hearing the boy's voice so clearly, at hearing him speak more than a sentence, and in this shock and in the relief of finding him, I do not fully understand the implication of his question: Is it true that my lord never told him why we were going on a journey? This seems impossible. Even so, surely Hiroko and I discussed the mission in front of the boy at some point during our trip, surely I myself or Hiroko directly spoke to the boy about it, but I cannot now remember a time when we did. I think back on what Hiroko said when we found the corpse, but I cannot now remember, either, whether the boy understood what Hiroko was talking about. I step forward and lean down a little toward the men to tell them to shut up, that I will be the one to explain all this to Yumi, when the one on the left stands and approaches me.

Before I can resist or draw my sword, he bows deeply and says, "Toshio-san, please," and gestures down the garden path away from the party. "Let them get to know each other."

The man, who is Korean, is perhaps my age and speaks perfect Japanese. I surmise he is an escort to the older one—the one we have been waiting for—and as discreetly as possible, I scan his robe to see any possible weapons he might be carrying. If he is, they are well hidden.

I have not taken my hand off the handle of my sword. I look back. I see that the boy is now sharing tea with the older Korean, the steam rising thinly above their shoulders into the morning.

"Please do not worry," the escort says, and once again bows deeply. He has neither introduced himself nor revealed how he knows my name, though I suppose it is obvious that Yumi told him. In another time, I would have treated this as wanton disrespect, but I know I must be patient, that I promised my lord I would safely deliver the boy to these people.

I begin to walk with him. He leads me out of the garden and back up the hill toward the stalls.

"The boy," the escort says. "Yumi. That is what you call him? That's a lovely name. In Korean, it can mean *beauty*. Girls are often named that." The escort chuckles. I stay silent. He goes on: "He is a fine boy. Yes, a fine boy. You raised him well. I mean, of course, not you, I apologize. You were in the war? Of course you were. Look at you. How we feared you. Now look at us both. Two old soldiers, yes? What are we doing here? This is my third trip to Japan. I have children of my own. A wife. I have not seen them in over a year, traveling around with old men, you name them, one after another coming here for whatever reason as though suddenly we are fast friends, my country and yours."

The escort chuckles again. He has not once looked at me but stays close to me, close enough, I know, to block my arm if I were to draw a sword. We have arrived at the stalls. Just then the old breeder appears from the side. Beside him on a leash is the dog that came up to me. The breeder bows and hands the leash to the escort.

"She is a loyal dog. She will make a good hunting dog. A thousand good wishes to you."

The breeder retreats, heading toward the teahouse. The aliveness of the animal shifts us both away from whatever circle the escort had been drawing around me. I steal a glance at the man as he gets on his knees and coos over the dog and says something to her in Korean. Some travelers stare at him, but stay silent.

"I thought the boy might like a dog," the escort says. "To help him. With the transition. These dogs do not have comparisons. Not even in Korea. Even I know this."

"He may not want a dog," I say, perhaps too quickly, because the escort glances up at me.

"Then I'll take the dog for myself," he says.

I feel his eyes staying on me as that heat flares up inside of me again. I turn and look back down at the teahouse, where the older Korean is talking intently to the boy, gesturing things with his hands, drawing something on his scroll.

"We're aware the boy doesn't speak Korean," the escort says. "The man over there. The one who will be taking him. He's a scribe. He speaks Japanese and several other languages. He'll teach the boy."

"Will Yumi always be with that man?" I say. "Will there be anyone else?"

The escort gets up, brushing the dirt from his pants, and shrugs. "I only know what I know: the scribe wanted a son. They'll travel. They'll travel for as long as the scribe can. All over. Manchuria. Russia. Here. Korea. That will be their life."

I imagine the boy's travels. The adventures he will go on. The possibility that I will indeed see him again in some future time when he is no longer a boy. Perhaps passing through a post station or in a city somewhere. As I imagine this, the sun seems to settle over the station; a slight breeze comes. I shut my eyes and tilt my head toward it.

"Do you miss the fighting?" I say without thinking, it just comes out.

Tugging on the leash a little as we begin to walk back down to the garden, he considers the question. But he doesn't answer. He says, "Your lord's daughter-in-law. The one in mourning. I was sorry to hear that. But even so, she took us to the theater one night, insisted upon it. She sat with us. She translated everything, even though we understood. She didn't miss a word. It was marvelous. The play was about a house builder who is no longer a house builder. He has known only the building of homes for so long that when it is no longer a part of him, he does not know who he is anymore. So he travels. He travels everywhere, looking for others who might instruct him on how to build another life. He just keeps going. That is how the play ends. With him going and going. By the way, what is her name? I apologize, but I cannot recall. Your lord's daughter-in-law. The one in mourning."

I realize that as the escort has been relating me this story, I have been holding my breath. There is nothing I want more than to answer him. And to ask how she is. I almost do, trying to recall the dream I had yesterday as we enter the teahouse's garden. But then I hear it before I understand what is happening. The familiar sound that Hiroko used to call a song: an arrow cutting through the air, fast and forceful enough so that when it enters the side of the dog, the dog is lifted up and away, which causes the leash to go taut and the escort to be yanked to the ground. The escort shouts. The dog howls, once, then begins to whimper, not yet on the ground, impaled by the arrow, her legs kicking ferociously in the air, her mouth chomping nothing, drool already falling down her neck. I spin around. All I see is the scribe who has taken off his hat, standing now, stunned, and a few others from the teahouse gasping and watching. Then the breeder rushes over, tripping on the path, his fall stopped by Hiroko, who holds him there, not understanding what is going on but understanding enough.

I try to ignore the dog whimpering but cannot. I pull out my sword and with my knee I slide the dog down against the earth, the arrow pushing through her as she looks up at me with those eyes of hers, her teeth bared, remembering me from yesterday, I know, as I stab her in the heart and it is done.

I check on the escort. I pick up his hat and help him up. Everyone is looking at him. He looks back at the dog.

"Was that intended for us?" he says.

I shake my head. I explain it is my fault. I got him different arrows. The boy is unused to them. The weight and the power. He was probably trying to impress the scribe.

"Are you certain?" the escort says.

"He is just a boy," I say. "He is a scared boy who didn't know why he was coming here and where he is going."

"Find him before the scribe changes his mind," the escort says sharply. "I'll take care of this."

I bow. I hurry out of the garden, ignoring the people watching us as the escort calls for Hiroko and the breeder to help.

I keep hearing the whimper.

5.

The boy stands against a wall in an alley not far from the entrance of the post station. A sign has been erected on the main path, along with towers of sand to indicate the arrival of a lord sometime later today. I kneel in front of him. I say, "Was it the new arrows? You weren't used to them, yes? You didn't see us, yes? You were just showing the man your bow and arrows?"

He doesn't respond.

"You never miss," I say.

Nothing.

"You said more words a moment before than I have heard all month and now you won't talk."

I desperately want him to explain himself. I feel that heat again, I cannot control it; this time it is like a fire moving through a forest inside of me, and I grab his arms and shake him.

I say, "You stupid boy, you are not from here," and keep shaking him.

I say, "Don't you see? This is your chance, we are trying to help you go back home," and keep shaking him.

I say, "Do you not remember? We took you. You had no say in this. We picked you up from the arms of your dead mother. We took you in like an animal and bathed you and fed you and dressed you up and made you shoot arrows into apples to make people laugh and feel a moment of joy. We pitied you. We don't even know how to speak your

PAUL YOON

language. You don't even know how to speak your language. We took that away from you. You should hate us. Why don't you hate us? You can now be who you should have been, with the people you should have always been with."

The more he lets me shake him, the harder I do it until I hear his head hit the wall. His face crumples as he falls into a ball on the ground.

My hands are trembling. It is like I woke only now and everything else this morning had been a dream. I lean over him, checking his head for a wound, but he is okay. I take off my swords. I sit against the wall and tuck him in between my legs with his back against my chest the way I would some nights when I was on guard duty and he could not sleep and would sneak out to find me. I hold him. He has not bathed in days and yet I think he still smells like himself, wonderfully. I know the shape of him better than I do my own. I will always know. Ten years. It seems like no time has passed at all.

"That story," I say, calmly now, quietly. "The one Hiroko told you yesterday. About the skeleton of the warrior and the tree growing in him. It wasn't true. He made that up. It isn't true. He saw no such thing."

A passerby walks by the alley but doesn't see us.

"But is it true," Yumi says, "that you are dying?"

For a moment, I do not understand what he means by this. For a moment, I am convinced he knows something about myself that I do not. Then I realize that he is talking about all of us. That the *bushi* are dying. Or turning into something else.

"What do you think of him?" I say. I am talking about the Korean scribe.

"I like him very much," Yumi says. "Did I kill the dog?"

His voice is strong and clear like a river at the end of winter.

"Yes," I say. "You killed the dog."

I can feel him turning my words over in his mind.

"You will have a good life," I say. "A long, good life. You will be a good man. You will be brave. You will carry honor."

"Will I see you again?" he says.

Still holding him between my legs, I tap the side of his head.

"Talk to me," I say. "When you miss me. When you are happy. When you are scared. Talk to me."

"I am never scared."

I smile a little.

"Come on then," I say, and after adjusting our kimonos, we walk back together to the garden.

6.

It is late in the afternoon now. The lord who is supposed to arrive at the post station has yet to. But they have opened up the hot spring beyond the ridge of the hill, and so Hiroko and I head there after saying good-bye to the Koreans and Yumi. Another dog follows them, Yumi holding the leash loosely as they navigate the horses. They are heading back to Edo, and from there the boy and his new guardian will begin their travels.

I do not see them depart, though Hiroko turns on occasion as we climb the hill. He is trying to lift my spirits. He says, "Toshio-san. I know what will kill you now. It isn't the sword. It's boredom."

He laughs. Then he begins to tell me about his exploits at the brothel, but I stop listening. I have not told him about the alley and what I did, which I have never done. He would shrug and say the boy deserved it, though I am not convinced he would fully believe that.

I am thinking of the escort and the things he said to me; I am thinking of Kakue—they are suddenly like a single stone rattling at the back
of my throat. I do not know how to reach the stone and break it apart.
I have spent my life building rooms in my mind to step in or to never
step in and it is as if I have built all the rooms wrong.

We undress in the hut near the hot spring. We put on thin robes and
take the path to the water, the rocks underneath us cold and rough.
Hiroko throws off his robe and steps quickly into the spring, shivering,
the mist on the surface parting as he wades to the far back. Whatever
piece of wall that crumbled has been swept up and fixed, and up here,
in this corner of the station, I see the beauty of what this place had
once been in its entirety, the water nestled against this hill, the sun
settled against the outcrop, the mist.

I only now notice the couple bathing nearby. Hiroko, who has
reached the far end of the spring, stares at the woman's breasts un-
ashamedly. His head is over the mist so that from where I am on the
near bank it appears as though his head is afloat, severed, leering at the
naked woman who is focused on her husband or lover, whoever he is.

To my surprise, Hiroko's expression changes; whatever desire has
been on his mind alters. The change is as swift as the shadow of a bird
on a field. Hiroko shuts his eyes and begins to cry. He lifts his hands out
of the water and buries his head into them and, as his shoulders shake,
he cries. It does not last long. He composes himself and then rests his
head against the far bank, his mouth slightly open, and faces the sky.

I am by a tree that has yet to flower. I take off my robe and kneel.
I push the mist away and collect some water with my left hand. Just as
the bathing woman pauses, noticing what a useless cup a hand makes
without a thumb, a butterfly appears, like a new thought, its wings
almost touching my shadow, but not quite.

CROMER

In New Malden, they owned a corner shop together. It was the place where you could get the gossip magazines and newspapers from Seoul. Then when everyone got smartphones, it became the place to get your smartphone cases. Cute cats, cows, and hippos. Gel pens too. The students picked up a few colors while they got their fizzy drinks or, when it grew warmer, waited their turn at the shaved ice machine Harry convinced his wife they should get. At first Harry wanted a pinball machine, and Grace had to tell him that was ridiculous. What kid played pinball these days?

Harry never minded the kids—kids helped him forget that they had woken up one day to find themselves in their mid-forties—but Grace went to the back whenever they came in. She said it was because of their voices that sounded to her like paper shredders and the fact that they always picked up a box of something and left it somewhere else. But Harry knew it was because years ago one of them had come up to the counter while Grace was arranging the pens and asked if they were really North Koreans and what that was like there and whether they had any health defects or bad teeth or were actually siblings or something.

It was a parent who had made a comment about them, maybe at dinner, maybe while passing the shop, and their kid had overheard.

This happened a few times over the years, would happen probably until they died.

Harry and Grace weren't North Koreans, not technically. But their fathers had defected together in the early seventies and then a month later found a home here in the large Korean community in southwest London that only grew larger as the decades went on. Grace's father found work as a delivery truck driver; Harry's at a home and garden shop where, later, Harry and Grace would roam the greenhouse, trying to learn the names of plants and flowers. If there was talk about the two men who had escaped from the North, the focus on them dimmed as the seasons and years went on because more and more escaped and came to New Malden. Their fathers both met and married South Korean women; they had children, Grace older than Harry by a year.

They had known each other all their lives, their marriage an eventuality they never really spoke about until it happened. As children, they stayed over in each other's apartments and their mothers cooked for them and they went to school together and fought over what to watch on the television and who could pedal the bicycle and who would sit on the seat. When they were older, they poked each other in the stomach over who stole the other's cigarettes, and they went to the park to smoke and to read bad sex scenes in novels to each other. They sneaked away to Wembley to watch the Freddie Mercury tribute concert, where Grace understood what it meant for your breath to be taken away when Annie Lennox opened her mouth to sing. Then as the years went on, they practiced their Korean because they were forgetting some words and phrases and they also wondered more and more about their fathers' childhoods because their fathers never spoke about their lives before this one.

One winter, he and Grace were two blocks away when an IRA bomb went off. Even from there, the force of it lifted Grace just enough into Harry's arms, like she was a parachute that had caught the wind. He remembered the strange, floating soft silence of it all. The ballooning of her red coat. Then the snow that wasn't snow but the dust of bricks that had been blown apart. And Grace suddenly tucked in his arms, which she told him later was the safest place she could ever imagine being.

He saw the unfolding map of them. He always had. It kept them going through the decades and through the success of the shop. What he didn't see coming was when they lost three of their parents within a period of two years. Harry's father of a brain aneurysm and his mother of cancer. Grace's father of a bad heart. Or a broken one, perhaps, after losing his friend, Harry's father.

Then Grace's mother decided she'd had it with New Malden. Grace and Harry were unaware that she had ever felt restless there. She moved to Arizona, where she had a cousin, and took almost nothing with her.

Harry wasn't a superstitious man, or for that matter a spiritual one, but with them gone, he believed in grief, in profound, dumbstruck grief. That slow, heavy, animal feeling was like a coat he could never take off. It altered the day's colors, the sounds. Every moment reminded him of his father. A woman walking by cradling a plant in a pot. A voice from the street corner. Some news report about North Korea. Grace's mother showing up with a list of things Harry and Grace could have if they wanted—an old photo album, clothes, an ashtray, an unopened bottle of whiskey, a bicycle.

He never told Grace this, but he was almost relieved when she—Grace's mother—announced that she was moving to Arizona. Every few months, she sent a postcard of the desert, which Grace taped to the side of the register and which he almost always forgot about until the next one came.

Harry thought maybe he would grow closer to Grace in some new way, now that it was just the two of them—that he would discover some different part of the map he had been carrying in his head. That eventually they would shed that coat and find some hobby to do together or make new friends here or see more of the ones they had gone to school with. Maybe they would save up some money and go on a holiday—go somewhere, even briefly, where no one knew anything about them, where they were anonymous.

But in the absence of their families, they grew more solitary, to the life outside their shop windows and to each other. And if someone were to ask him why, or how, he didn't know. He would look up from the counter to find the afternoon almost gone and that if Grace had vanished he would not have noticed. It was as if the days and all the hours in those days hardened into a ring around them. He kept waiting for something to duck under the perimeter and reveal itself.

They drove to work, opened the shop, stayed until closing, sold what they sold, received shipments, cleaned the floors, wiped the counter, kept the books, took turns eating lunch in the back room, had to call the police a few times a month for the drunks or the people who wouldn't leave.

Nothing changed. In their bedroom one night, he turned on his side, exhausted, and, not for the first time, startled himself with the understanding that the woman beside him was the only person left in the immediate circle that could be called his family. Maybe their decision not to have children had been wrong. Was it too late for that?

Grace laughed.

"But that doesn't mean we can't try," he said, and winked at her.

"Did you just wink at me?" Grace said.

What was she always looking at online? He wondered how often their fathers thought about the place they had left behind. Whether they had truly been happy here and whether they'd had good marriages and were able to ignore the South Koreans who said things to them and to their wives because of who they were—whether they got over the inevitable scuffles and the word *Communist* spray-painted across their cars. Whether they ever regretted having children. And what came into their minds in the moment when they died. If anything came at all.

"Let me die first," Harry said, more than once, and Grace always replied, "I don't think so."

He started giving away the gel pens, trying to remember all the kids' names, what the gossip was, what they thought was cool, what movies and TV shows to watch.

If he tried too hard, he couldn't remember his father's face. It came to him only when he didn't try.

He had dreams of flowers whose names he kept forgetting. Enormous flowers Grace carried away across a wide river, almost tripping as she kept saying, "I don't think so."

●

Harry was closing up the shop one fall night when the bell rang and the door swung open. At first he thought it must be one of the local kids, because it was a kid. He had his hoodie up, so Harry didn't see the blood at first. Then the kid turned under the shop's lights. His nose was pretty banged up. The blood was coming down over his lips, which the kid kept licking like he was a dog.

Harry reached for him, but the kid flinched. Harry said, "All right. All right. I'm Harry. This is my shop." He spoke in Korean, wondering if the kid would understand. He did.

"What's your name?" Harry said, when the kid didn't respond.

"I don't know," the kid said.

He was twelve, probably. At most thirteen.

"I can't," the kid said, "I can't remember."

Grace walked in from the back. She had been dumping out the bucket of water and was holding the mop. The kid froze and Harry assured him it was okay, that she was his wife.

They had planned to see a movie that night and go out to dinner, something they hadn't done in a long time. He had even made a reservation at the sushi place they had gone to for her birthday one year, the one with the corner booth in the back with the curtains that made her feel like they were celebrities.

It was dark outside, and the three of them were reflected on the window, standing still.

"We should take care of that," Harry said.

The kid wiped his nose with the sleeve of his hoodie and winced.

"Let's get you away from the windows," Harry said, and reached for his arm again. This time, the kid let him. Harry guided him down an aisle into the back room, Grace looking at them the whole time, still holding the mop as she locked the front door.

Harry sat the kid down. He pressed a handkerchief against the kid's nose and told him to tilt his head back. He asked if there was anything he remembered, and the kid nodded and motioned for Harry's phone.

The kid dialed. Harry could hear the woman on the other end pick up and begin to scream hysterically. The kid nodded a lot and repeated that he couldn't remember as though the woman were there with them. The kid asked Harry where they were and he said, "New Malden, southwest London." And then gave him the street corner where the shop was. The kid repeated everything back and then hung up and paused. He looked up at Harry. He said when he dialed and was talking to the woman, he knew the person was his mother, but now he wasn't sure anymore.

"Who else would it be?" Harry said.

The kid rubbed his head and then tilted his head back again. He said he had never felt so confused. He said things were coming back to him, but it was like the things were a step away always, knowing he was trying to reach for them.

Two policemen arrived. Grace had called. Harry thought the kid would try to run but he didn't. He glanced back at them and slid down the chair, holding his nose, and shut his eyes.

Harry went with him to the hospital. The kid gave him the number he had dialed, and Harry left a message for the woman about where they were going. He stayed at the hospital for three hours, keeping the boy talking, answering the policemen's questions, listening to the policemen ask the kid questions.

The kid's nose was broken, and a nurse had bandaged it up. One of the policemen had asked if the kid had been in a car. He said the nose injury indicated a possible car accident. The head trauma would have caused the partial memory loss. He asked if the kid was driving.

All the kid kept saying was "Cromer." He thought he lived in Cromer.

"On the sea?" Harry said.

The policeman jotted something down in his notepad.

Cromer was where Harry and Grace had gone on their honeymoon. The owner of the Korean restaurant down the street had a cousin who worked at a seaside hotel and had gotten them a discount. They spent hours on the boardwalk and visited the pubs and shopped. It was grand.

He wondered if the kid knew the restaurant owner in some way, if that was why he had ended up in New Malden. He said the man's name but the kid shook his head.

It was then the kid's mother arrived. She was much younger than Harry had imagined, in her early thirties and wearing the same hoodie as the boy. She came up to Harry and said, "Thank you, thank you, thank you," and began to cry. She smelled like a strong shampoo. She showed the police her license and then a photo of the kid in her purse.

"Cromer," the policeman said, handing back her ID.

"Ten quid," the policeman whispered to Harry as they watched the reunion. "Ten quid says it was the father. Took the boy. Got drunk. Crashed somewhere. We'll find the car and then the man."

It was clear the kid recognized her, but couldn't quite place her. Still, he hugged her back and they stayed like that for a while, their bodies like a giant clamshell on the bed.

When Harry went back to the shop, it was almost one in the morning. On the street, a taxi drove by and then two girls in skirts walked down the sidewalk, swaying their hips and twirling glow sticks.

Grace was where he had left her, mopping the floors. He told her she had already done that. She yawned, rubbed her eyes with her knuckles. She asked about the kid. He wanted to say something about the movie and the dinner they had planned but his throat was raw, his body suddenly as heavy as a potato sack. The radio switched to a commercial, the shop filling with the hurried sound of language like birdsong, and Harry reached over and unwrapped the mop from Grace's fingers.

•

Harry never found out who the kid was or what exactly had happened to him. He didn't know if there had indeed been a father or a car, if they ever found a car. He looked for news online about a neighborhood incident the following day and the whole week but there was nothing mentioned. He even asked a policeman who stopped in, a different one, who wanted a coffee. Harry explained. The policeman picked up a few of the pens on the counter and said that he was sorry, it wasn't his case, but that it seemed Harry had done everything right.

Harry wasn't sure what the policeman meant.

Grace was better at finding things on the internet, but she came up with nothing as well. "Forget about it," she said, and moved on to whatever it was she was watching on her phone in bed.

Maybe Harry himself had watched too many of those TV shows the kids liked lately. He felt a small knot inside him he wanted to pick at but couldn't reach. He wondered if the kid's memory had come back. He wondered if the father was sick or into drugs or both. When Harry was a child, a man had approached his father one day and asked if he was "right in the head." He was delivering plants to the restaurant down the street the day before it opened and he had dropped a box. It wasn't the box, though, but because his father hardly spoke and people wondered if he was mute.

What was right about the head? Harry thought.

The next day, Harry asked Grace to cover for him and walked down to the restaurant on the same street as their shop. The owner, John, was sitting at a table, preparing takeout kits, placing chopsticks and napkins into plastic bags. If he was surprised to see Harry, he didn't show it. Harry himself was surprised to find that John's hair had grown more gray. How long had it been? John had lived not far from the home and garden shop—he had even gone to the Freddie Mercury tribute concert with them—but they hadn't seen much of each other since Grace's mother left for Arizona.

Harry brought up the cousin.

"He's no longer working at the hotel," John said.

He proceeded to tell Harry that his cousin had slipped on a step last winter and shattered his hip. The hotel couldn't keep him on, so he had gone farther north, to York. "We send him what we can," John said.

He asked if Harry was looking to get a deal at the hotel again, but Harry didn't go on. Instead, he flipped through the menu and ordered lunch for Grace, pretending not to notice that John was looking at him. He knew John was wondering why they hadn't come by in a while, not even for a dinner at the restaurant. He waited for John to say something like he was angry, upset, or confused, but John only smiled and kept going with his takeout kits.

Harry sat down by the window. Shadows panned across the sunny floor between them like the carousel at the nearby park they used to go to as children. As he watched the shadows, it suddenly seemed to Harry as though he had been sitting here for many hours, as though it was much later in the day than he assumed it was.

"You look tired, Harry," John said. "You're working too much."

"I'm all right," Harry said.

The smell of hot cooking oil drifted in from the kitchen. Harry leaned forward and took some of the napkins and chopsticks to place inside the plastic bags.

"Does this have something to do with the boy last week?" John said.

"He was from Cromer," Harry said.

"They say he was a runaway," John said.

"Who says?" Harry handed John a few of the kits he had finished.

"They say he lost his memory before he got to where he wanted to go," John said. "And now he must be back home with no idea of why he was running away in the first place. Or from whom." John took some more kits from Harry and laughed. "Imagine us in front of Wembley, forgetting why we were there at all and turning back around."

"She seemed all right," Harry said. "The mother. I don't think he would do that."

"Man, Annie Lennox," John said. "Break your fucking heart. Bowie too, of course. But really, no contest. Look at my arm. Chills just thinking about it."

Harry scratched his own arm. He thought about what John had

heard. He remembered the mother, who he admitted to himself was pretty, and the way she kept saying thank you to him.

Then the food was ready. They gave Harry extra rice. John said to give Grace a hello. And then he said that they should both come to the next bingo night, and Harry said that they would and returned to the shop.

•

He thought it would stay with him the way certain things did. A man asking his father whether he was right in the head; Grace in his arms as building debris fell on them like snow; the greenhouse in the nights; the spray paint on the cars. But the truth was that as time passed, whatever had been caught inside him got dislodged and fell. Harry stopped thinking about the boy or his mother and that night. Or if the memory surfaced, he no longer lingered on it the way he had done that first week.

No other news of it ever came through the shop and no one, not even Grace, ever spoke of it again. The shop kept them busy enough that the days sped by. A few months later, they had a mishap with a large order—the delivery truck never arrived—and their life was consumed by the fallout for a week, as they tracked down the delivery, made phone calls, handled the complaining customers, were faced with the money lost. He expected the stress to boil over and that he or Grace would start a fight or shout or walk away, which was how they always dealt with stress.

But that never happened. They shared a laugh. They rolled their eyes at each other over a customer who considered it a disaster not to have milk. They said there was nothing to do tonight and closed early and finally went to a movie, a comedy about a small-town girl in America heading into the city.

The holidays came, which was always a boon for them, the way they sold out of things they never sold out of, like gift wrapping paper and scissors and those glow-in-the-dark stickers intended for children, all the partygoers stopping in on their way to somewhere else. For New Year's Eve, they headed over to the community center, playing bingo and watching the new season of a Korean historical drama until John shouted what losers they were and began a dance party.

They played Queen, of course. Harry thought Grace looked beautiful there, a little drunk, attempting to keep up with John as the two of them sang along and avoided the small puddles the melting snow from their boots had made. He thought the decades hadn't been that long at all. He could still see them sneaking into the greenhouse one night as children because Grace was convinced something happened to plants when they slept. How they fell asleep under a tarp before they could notice anything, and how his father found them an hour later, worried sick.

It was the only time his father had ever struck him. "You never run away," his father said, on his knees, and then struck Harry again, quickly, the moon bright in the greenhouse and his father only a silhouette.

Grace was the one who brought up Cromer early that following year. She was behind the counter and scrolling through a travel site on her phone. Her birthday was coming up. Winter also meant the off-season and they could find a good deal. They hadn't gone on a holiday in years, but at the community center, while dancing drunk, they had promised each other that if they remembered this conversation, then they would close up the shop for two days.

They remembered. It was a New Year's resolution, although they'd heard no one called it a resolution anymore. Was that true?

"How about Cromer?" she said, and he wondered if she remembered the boy. He had told her about how the boy kept saying that word over and over until his mother showed up. Harry reminded Grace about it now, and she said, "My god, I haven't thought about that in ages. Whatever happened to him?"

Harry didn't know. Grace made a sound with her lips. She scrolled down and said the hotel they had stayed at for their honeymoon was still too expensive for them but that she'd found another, smaller one a little farther down.

"But still across the boardwalk," Grace said, and smiled.

Harry wiped down the drip tray of the shaved ice machine. He wrote a reminder to himself to do inventory tomorrow.

"That's what you want?" Harry said.

"That's what I want," Grace said.

•

They drove up at the end of the month. They notified everyone in the neighborhood and everyone asked when they would finally hire help so that the shop could stay open on days they left. Harry and Grace promised to consider it, and then they considered it on the drive up, promising each other to finally start looking.

"Any one of those kids who come into the shop," Harry said, and Grace rolled her eyes. They had stopped for lunch in Norwich. He had mentioned that they needed to order more biscuits and Grace made him promise that was the last thing he would say about the shop until they returned. They clinked their beers and ordered too much, so by the time they arrived at Cromer the thought of dinner seemed impossible.

They didn't want to waste the holiday, however, and figured if they walked a bit through the town, their appetites would return. They bundled up in their parkas and gloves and headed inland first, following a windy narrow road with squat, two-story buildings painted different colors.

Grace was trying to recall a ceramics shop they had stepped into on their honeymoon. They had bought dinner plates there. She thought maybe they could add to the collection. She checked her phone, but couldn't remember the name. Maybe it was a block away from where they were, but there was only a souvenir shop there, next to one that sold clothes. They browsed coats in the window, Harry following Grace's reflection, the pale puff of her breath. She caught him looking. For some reason he was embarrassed, and he looked away.

They didn't find the shop, but they found the fish and chips place they had eaten at almost every day. The small, half-filled dining room stared at them as they found a table. They ignored the stares and reminisced about their honeymoon and remembered the church and the small park where they sat, sharing an ice cream. Then they remembered an argument they'd had about whether or not to head down to Great Yarmouth, Harry telling her what difference did it make, a coastal town was a coastal town.

Grace smiled. Now, years later, she confessed that maybe that was true, maybe he had been right. Behind her, the man kept glancing at them. Harry glanced back and then asked if Grace was bored here. She shook her head.

"I'm sorry," Grace said, reaching across the table. "I didn't mean that."

He said it was all right. He turned to the window where some large birds were flying out to sea.

"Something on your mind, Harry?"

"It's better than I remember it," Harry said, tearing open the fried fish with his hands and dipping it in the sauce.

Grace's father had liked fried fish. He mentioned this: every time he had fried fish, he thought of Grace's father.

"Did you ever see them fight?" Harry said, taking another bite.

"What?"

"I don't remember our dads ever fighting. They always got along."

"They did."

"They were too polite to each other."

"Don't be absurd, Harry."

The waiter came by, and they ordered another round of beers.

"I'd like to have seen them as children," Harry said. "In their village. I bet they got into some nasty fights. Children aren't polite. That's what I like about them."

"They were half dead," Grace said. "And when they made it here years later, they were more than half. They never caught up to being alive. That was their life. Catching up to everyone else. You know better, Harry."

"What is it about children that you don't like?"

Grace put down a chip. He could see her inhale and then exhale. And then she reached across and held his hand, squeezing a little.

"I don't know where this is going, Harry."

Another couple walked in. Their beers arrived and music began to play quietly on the speaker.

He didn't know where he was going with this either. As he squeezed her hand back, he noticed the man behind Grace had gone. They finished their dinner, listening to the music.

A light snow began to fall on the seaside town. They were going to walk some more but they headed back to the hotel, passing the larger one they had stayed in, where John's cousin used to work. They peered through the revolving door at the bright lobby, wondering if anything had changed, but when a bellhop welcomed them, they grew shy about it and kept going down parallel to the boardwalk and the ocean across from them.

The snow never grew heavier but remained steady enough to dampen their jackets. It wasn't unpleasant. He could taste it when in the small hotel room she leaned up to kiss him and then the smell of it was everywhere as they undressed. It was like he was drunk on the snow and not the beer. He laughed, louder than he usually did. He was glad to be here. It was good of them to have come up here again.

Afterward, as they lay on the bed together, Grace's hair dampening the sheet, Grace began to dream. He could hear her talking but couldn't make out what she was saying. He watched her mouth move in shapes and then, giving in to an urge, he stuck his finger inside, gently, feeling her lips graze his fingertip. Her mouth moving like that aroused him. He looked down at her soft belly and the maze of veins on her thigh, growing convinced she wasn't really asleep, and then realizing she really was.

What was she dreaming of? What lives did she live these days, or hope to live, that she didn't tell him about?

Grace rolled to her side, pulled the blanket over herself in her sleep. The room had grown cold. Harry stood to check the electronic thermostat only to find it wasn't working. He pulled on his pajamas and threw on the hotel robe.

"I'll be right back," he said, knowing she wouldn't answer, and shut the door as quietly as possible behind him.

In the lobby, he mentioned the thermostat, and when the receptionist said that she would get someone up there right away, he hesitated. He didn't want to wake Grace. He said, "We have an extra blanket. It's fine, it's late, how about tomorrow?"

He had no idea what time it was. He was the only one in the lobby. He was about to head back up but found himself stepping outside instead. The snow had stopped. A thin layer covered the street and the sidewalk. He luxuriated in the cold and listened to the ocean waves. It was so quiet that it was as though the world had vanished. As though he and Grace were the last people left behind. How would he feel about that?

He was thinking of this when he spotted the figure on a boardwalk bench. The figure was wearing a hoodie and on occasion would turn and look down at the pier and the ocean.

Harry crossed the street. When the kid looked up, Harry immediately knew it wasn't the kid he was looking for.

"I'm sorry," he said. "I thought you were someone else."

"Who did you think I was?" the kid said.

Harry thought about that. "Someone I met," he said.

"You a perv or something?" He eyed Harry's robe. "I don't swing like that."

Harry shook his head, aware that shaking his head was ridiculous. He explained he was a guest at the hotel but then wondered if he should have said that. A car drove by, the headlights lighting them up briefly. If the kid was frightened, he didn't show it. When Harry asked what the kid was doing here, the kid replied, "This is my spot." He opened the duffel beside him and asked if Harry was interested in the goods: inside were counterfeit watches and sunglasses, cigarettes, jewelry, and small plastic bags of something Harry didn't recognize.

Harry looked around. At the end of the pier, a bird landed on the railing like it was balancing itself at the edge of the world, looking down at the receding water.

"It's not a very popular time or place," Harry said.

"I can be here anytime I want," the kid said. "I can float like a butterfly. I can sting like a bee. Every day is free. You free, old man?"

He wasn't sure how to answer that. He wasn't used to people calling him old.

The kid opened one of the small plastic bags, picked up one of the things inside, shook it, and it began to glow. It looked like a cartoon drawing of a star. "It's for the children," the kid said. "They love it." He inserted the star into a plastic gun of some kind and then aimed up above them and fired. Harry followed it as the glowing star shot up into the sky, going higher than he thought it would, and then floated slowly back down, swaying a little in the wind. Harry took three steps to the right, opened his hand, and caught it.

When he looked back down, the bird had gone. As Harry returned the star to the kid, he asked if he was from here and whether he had heard about a runaway last year.

"A Korean boy," Harry said. "Twelve, thirteen, about the same age as you."

"Mate," the kid said. "You're shivering bad."

He tightened his robe and blew into his hands. Out on the water, near the dark horizon, a small vessel was speeding across like it was sliding on glass. Where was it going? He didn't know suddenly what lay directly east of them, across the sea. Or how long it would take a small boat to get there to that other coast. He had never been anywhere outside of England. Neither had Grace.

"What's next?" Harry said. "What happens next for me?"

Ignoring him, the kid stared behind Harry at another kid, a girl who had just walked out of the hotel Harry had stepped out from. She zipped up her puffer, waved, and crossed the street.

"Hi," she said to Harry, or the kid, Harry wasn't entirely sure, her breath ballooning around them as she stuffed her hands into her jacket pockets and hopped in place.

The kid pulled down his hoodie and fixed his hair. Then his face softened.

"I'll look out for your boy," he said, and before Harry could correct him or figure out their story, the two of them hurried up the board-walk together, going farther and growing fainter—another star flying up into the distance, the moonlight playing on the water, all their foot-prints in the snow.

THE HIVE AND THE HONEY

South Ussuri, Primorsky Krai, 1881 April Report

Dear Uncle,

About the recent tragic and mysterious events here in your outpost, I can now relate this:

Thirty-four days ago, in the middle of the night, I was woken by a loud noise coming from the Korean settlement. It sounded like a drum or a tree falling. Or so I thought because I was dreaming of Father, who you may recall liked to bang two sticks together to keep rhythm when your family played music after dinner. In the dream, however, he was not young but looked the way I imagine he would look if he were with us today: a trim, gray beard and missing his jaw from the Ottoman bullet, but very much alive.

Did you know in other dreams I find that jaw and carry it? Do you dream of such things about your brother?

In any case, I threw on my coat, grabbed my rifle, and hurried down the hill. I was concerned one of their *fanzas* might have collapsed, or that a bear had come, or both. They are ingenious, those houses—they are, as I learned, in the traditional style of their country with covered windows that protect them from the million biting flies that have altered my skin, and they contain a heating system that keeps the floor and seating area warm during the winters. But a bear, of course, if provoked, could tear down the door or a window and get in.

There was no bear that I could see. I counted all the rooftops as I kept going. The moon was high and bright and everywhere. Grass sparkled. All the *fanzas* were there. It was when I was closer that I noticed a door open to the one nearest to the river. A crowd of about thirty had gathered in front but no one had gone closer yet.

I made my way through them easily and spotted the man of the house lying halfway out of the space—he was shuddering a little like the last moments of those fish you used to teach me how to catch, and he was clutching his throat. Someone was trying to help and clutching his throat as well.

In the moment I understood what was happening and saw that his body was covered in a dark wetness, I heard more footsteps behind me, more doors opening—the sound I had heard was of a door banging open—and the man stopped shuddering and went completely motionless. There was a collective gasp. The night air cold enough at the start of spring for our breaths to appear in the moonlight.

Then the man's wife appeared from the house, stepped over her husband's dead body, and walked out to the grass and faced everyone and lifted the bloody knife she was holding and said in Korean—the neighbor next to me translated as best he could—that her husband tried to take advantage of her as she slept and hit her when she refused him, and hit her again, and she got so tired of it, all of it, every night, every single night, so tired of it, and there, it was done. She threw down the knife. She stared at everyone. And then at me. Her hair was wild. But she wasn't scared.

"You're married," someone shouted at her from the crowd. "What's there to take advantage of, you bitch?"

There was silence. And then the man who had been trying to help save the husband, his arms all covered in blood—he turned out to be the man's brother—walked up to his sister-in-law, picked up the knife, and struck her in the head with the handle, once, but hard enough for her to crumple like an ancient twig.

I rushed toward him, or tried to, but I was held. I reminded the men holding me that I was the police to this settlement and that they were under Russian governance, but whether they understood me or cared I didn't know. They gripped harder the harder I struggled as the brother waved the knife at me and approached and said, in broken Russian, that I had no business here, that this was a family matter, and when I reminded him of who I was, he said, "You are a useless Cossack who is young enough to be drinking his mother's breast milk, who has done nothing here and will do nothing here, ever, and if you say another word we will do to you what I am about to do to my bitch sister."

He said this and spat and took my rifle and yelled, or it was more of a bellow. He headed to his house. He came out with a large rope meant for an animal and wrapped one end around his sister-in-law's neck. At the weight of this and the motion, she woke, but before she could struggle, he was already pulling her toward the tree by the river.

The rest happened quickly. I shouted. I tried to break free once more, but I was no match for the men holding me. The brother threw the rope over the thickest branch, and with the rope over his shoulder he began to walk away from the water. The woman was dragged into the water first, submerged for a moment, and then was lifted. I thought our eyes met again until I realized she was looking just beyond me.

So I looked away in that direction as she died, to where her daughter of around twelve years had come out, the daughter who would later gesture to me, as I knew she would, that she had heard nothing, didn't know what had happened, because she couldn't hear, was born unable to hear, she was asleep, she was dreaming.

"What were you dreaming about?" I said in Russian. She had stopped crying and was reading my lips.

Music, she gestured, pretending to play a stringed instrument.

•

That was the beginning. I was never given my rifle back, but I was let go and told to leave them alone, that I was no police here.

"Leave us in peace," they said.

"What peace?" I said, pointing first at the man with his throat slit and then at the body hanging from the tree.

Still, I went back up, peering down on occasion at what had transpired below, which alternated between shadow and the moonlight.

Am I a coward for staying up there for the rest of the night? For doing nothing to stop this from happening? Do you think me a coward, Uncle? Your orders after my preliminary years were to dispatch me to this remote region a world away from you where I would report on the goings-on of a) a newly formed Korean settlement of about fifteen houses, and b) the area in general.

And when I asked what exactly you meant by the "goings-on," you didn't respond. You passed me the reins of one of your horses, which I know you weren't supposed to do—was that an act of kindness, or love?—and handed me a matchlock rifle, told me that every thirty or so days a messenger would come to pick up my report, and finally thanked me for my honorable service.

So here is my report, my third, and yet no messenger has come.

I am Andrei Bulavin, twenty-two years old, your nephew and son of Petro Timofeyevich, who died valiantly in the Balkans, and this is my fourth year of service under your command. I have received the highest level as a marksman and as a swordsman, in leadership, penmanship, cartography, languages; I can save a horse's life a dozen different ways, can build shelters, estimate wind speed, build a fire faster than anyone else in the barracks. . . . Is this a punishment?

The body remained hanging in the tree all night. Then, in the morning, I watched the daughter use an ax to cut her mother down. She plummeted into the water and for a moment the daughter, as though unprepared for what to do next, watched her mother float and twist and roll down the water until she got tangled in an old beaver dam. Then she dragged her mother out and proceeded to dig two graves near her house. No one helped. She grew tired. She kept digging.

I dressed in my uniform and came back down, this time on Timo, and I helped her as my horse drank the river water and grazed. Neighbors watched but did nothing. We wrapped the bodies in blankets but the daughter changed her mind, I think because she would have no more blankets. She covered her parents' faces with some of their clothes instead and we buried them and I said that I was sorry.

But I forgot she couldn't hear me, so I faced her and said it again, in Russian, and then in Korean—I had been learning as much as I could—and after a moment she drew what I believed was my matchlock on the dirt. I shook my head. I said, "Someone here has it. There are too many of them." She considered this. I nodded and said that I was indeed in a predicament, but I didn't think she knew I was talking.

Timo came up to her and softly pushed his head against her. This made her smile. She was thin and short for her age and I could not read her at all, what held her now, what passed through, whether it was sadness or anger or both or none of this. I knew she wanted little to do with her uncle, and her uncle wanted nothing to do with her. She was an orphan and was now living alone in a *fanza* that her parents had built a world and a lifetime away from where she was born, a house that was now hers.

My third month here, and I had already forgotten her name, had seen her twice perhaps before last night, was too embarrassed now to ask for it again. I had spent these past months speaking to as many of these settlers as I could, as many as would speak to me, but my picture of them wasn't complete: I gathered that most had come from a province just across the border that had been suffering from drought. There were no children—except the daughter who had just lost her parents—though it wasn't clear whether there had once been children in their community elsewhere and whether there were plans for families to begin. Many of them were older than I thought they would be, in the latter half of their lives. Two were wanted thieves who had escaped from a penal colony in Manchuria, a man of an ancient age mentioned matter-of-factly, offering me some of the tobacco he was smoking.

No one cared. Just as no one cared at first why I had come here and what role I was to play for them as long as I wasn't a hindrance to their daily lives. They resided together peacefully and worked together and grew barley and buckwheat and corn. It wasn't technically their land; they were tenant farmers for a Russian landowner who now lived in Vladivostok and who had given up trying to cultivate this land.

They weren't the only ones. There were pockets of them all over, these small Korean settlements scattered up and down the valley.

Are these the goings-on you would like to know about? That they are entirely self-sufficient, seem to be immune to these dreaded flies that have scarred my face, that they have built better houses than ours even in the Cossack lands or those belonging to the indigenous tribes? That they have succeeded where Russians weren't able to by cultivating this land, that they ferment vegetables by digging down far into the earth? That they are private and say little, but many of them already know Russian, and that there seems to be a school being built somewhere north at a larger settlement?

There is even a missionary who moves from one settlement to the next, selling products from a horse-drawn cart and briefly saying a sermon before he moves on. I have spent time with him, have bought wares from him, a pot of honey, a hammock I can hang over the stove in the winter to sleep in warmth.

That was where I was when the next disturbances started. The cold came back for a few days, and I had hung the hammock back up above the stove and was drifting off when I heard someone scream. In my disorientation and tiredness, I forgot what had befallen the settlement and the mess I had made of things. I put on my boots and flung on my coat, reached for the matchlock that wasn't there, remembered, hurried down.

Timo the war-horse, whom I had left with the daughter to keep her company, upon recognizing me grew excited, but I told him to stay where he was in front of the house. The screaming was coming from elsewhere. Other members of the settlement had come out. Together we headed into the brother's house, the one who had hung his sister-in-law.

We found him clutching a blanket and staring off into the distance somewhere beyond his wall. His skin was as pale as ash.

"She's not dead!" he shouted, and bit the blanket like a child.

•

I attempted to lead the investigation into this matter, which in truth I thought of as no matter at all. The drunken murderer was having nightmares. I thought: perhaps if he kept having them, he would eventually depart. Good riddance. He was no uncle, either. I should say I had yet to see them interact. More than once, I have heard him call her "the runt" or "the deaf bitch."

I know in my heart that with one stab of my saber, he is gone swiftly and efficiently, but I feel ill at ease doing so without your permission. Do I have your permission? Will you ever read this? Have I entered a lawless land only to eventually become lawless myself? What is it that you want me to do?

The settlement wanted me at first to do nothing. They decided to take charge themselves and at sunrise they helped the brother dig up the bodies once more. They were both there, the bodies. Already rotting. The clothes the daughter had used to cover their faces ruined now from the digging up.

The brother began to shake. "I swear to you," he said. "She came back."

As far as everyone could tell, the case was closed. Everyone returned to their work. The following evening, just as the sun set, more screaming was heard. This time from another house. Another man was clutching his blanket and staring at his wall and shouting, "Oh please, oh please, oh please, this isn't happening."

When one of the farmers asked the man to describe what exactly he saw, he said "a woman with brightness like fire" and "full of vengeance" approached him before vanishing. (Again, someone obliged and translated this for me.) I wanted to ask how one saw the manifestation of vengeance, but I kept my mouth shut. I thought: someone was playing a cruel joke. Or perhaps it wasn't cruel at all. I quite liked it, in fact. I was impressed. Good riddance.

I also considered that they were eating too much of the "drunken" bread they make and were having a collective delirium propelled by guilt. They had punished a woman defending herself and sided with the actions of a rapist.

I sneaked away as they kept talking and headed to the daughter's house. Timo was by the front door, standing guard. I nuzzled his face. I slid open the door slightly to find the girl in deep sleep, wearing her nightclothes, her hair fanned out across the wooden floor, the room undisturbed.

•

Now it is day thirty-five after the deaths of the parents. Almost every member of the settlement has been visited by what they are calling the apparition. It's never the husband, always the wife. They describe her in the exact same way. A moving brightness. Anger. The same height and shape as the hanged woman.

It has gone on long enough that I believe other settlements have now heard about it. The missionary has stopped visiting. I no longer see the faint silhouettes of riders on a far ridge. Not even, it seems, the bears want to tread here.

Only the birds keep coming. Hundreds of them. Silent until something startles them and they explode from the river tree as if all the branches have burst.

The day I left for this post, you said, "Be aware and afraid of bandits."

There are no bandits here. Maybe there were once. Probably someday there will be again. For now, it is only ourselves.

You see, we seem to have become the fear. The settlers try to stay up, afraid to shut their eyes. The settlement has also assigned rotating sentries and they all take turns making their rounds at night. It doesn't matter. Someone always sees the woman. Now it has been long enough that some have seen her more than once.

They have formed a council of some kind to talk about this ghost, but also, I infer, to discuss other matters pertaining to the land and their homes.

I find these two-headed strands of conversation fascinating. They want to solve the present situation but also to solve, apparition aside, the never-ending hurdle that is the future here for them.

Even through all this, they seem determined to enter it.

Sometime during the unease of these days, my matchlock vanished. I know this because the brother approached me and accused me of taking it back. I almost reached for my sword. I almost brandished it and pointed it at him the way he pointed the knife at me. I told him that he could check my house if he wanted, but he waved his arms, walked away, and then turned.

I expected the burst of anger I was accustomed to from him, but to my surprise his face had grown soft and sincere and broken, and he said calmly, "Please leave us alone. We are trying to live in a land no one wants or thinks about. Everything was fine until you came here, wanting it again."

I find that hard to believe. That everything was fine.

I have deduced that it is possible someone is lighting the fuse of my matchlock to present a "brightness." That there is impressive trickery here. But who is it?

I have tactfully begun to speak to those willing to speak to me, the way I began to do when I first came here, but there are few who believe this is not a supernatural event. They believe they are being punished for their role in the woman's death and this is now the way of things.

"So we scream," they say. "We lose sleep. There's still the next day, isn't there?"

When I ask them if perhaps they should leave a haunted place, that I would be happy to search for another plot of land, that they have all left once for somewhere else and succeeded—when I ask them all this, they all respond with some three-hundred-year-old story about a

Japanese invasion and then the history of temples and missionaries and European ships and that a ghost is nothing.

They say, "So we scream. We lose sleep. It's not killing us. Why should we leave?"

"You're the police," they say, finally. "Get rid of the ghost."

Only two people have remained untouched by this: myself and the daughter. The settlement seems to think this is logical. Why would the mother haunt her daughter? Or haunt the one person who attempted to defend her? No one seems to consider me as the perpetrator for obvious reasons. But the fact that no one seems to consider the daughter is curious to me. I know that neither her height nor her hair length match her mother's. But perhaps she has figured out a way to alter her appearance so that the settlement believes she is her mother. That is possible.

No one attempts to speak to her. No one acknowledges her as she passes to work her bit of land on her own or to visit her parents. Has it always been this way, all these years, long before I came? In their discrimination, have they failed to see her intelligence, her maturity, and that in a month's time she has lost both her parents? If she is tormenting them, I do not blame her. But for how long will she do so? I have tried many times to bring it up in a way I feel is appropriate but have failed to do so every time.

So it is a great surprise when one afternoon she walks up to my post, leading Timo. She unwraps the blanket she has been using as a bag and places food she has prepared into tiny bowls and scatters them around us on the floor like a game we are about to play. She begins to eat. She gestures for me to join her, so I do and I eat with her. We eat it all. Every last spoonful. Then she lies down and shuts her eyes. I poke her and point up to the hammock and she climbs up and in, and I light the fire underneath, and she falls asleep. I lie down on the floor and listen to her breathing, thinking that she cannot hear herself ever.

What is a heartbeat to someone who cannot hear it? What is breathing?

Could Father hear himself before he breathed his last breath?

A buzzing flashes over me. For a moment I brace myself, waiting for the woman to appear for the first time in this house, but it is only a bee that has managed to find its way inside. I watch as it flits about, on the scent of something, and then it settles into my teacup where I used the last of my honey today.

It is then I realize, privately, that today is my birthday. Did she know this, and therefore visited and shared a meal with me? That is impossible.

I know nothing. That is how I feel just then. I know fire and horses and how to write and I miss my father.

I am wondering when this will end—and what will be here in a season, a year, ten years—when I hear another scream. The girl shifts in the hammock as I feed the fire.

The night is full.

•

Early next morning, a few of the farmers are outside when I step out to relieve myself. A woman and three men. The woman speaks Russian. A man translates for the others. She shakes her head at me and says that I am a disgusting man for taking to bed with a child and that I am no different than the murdered man.

She says, "Have you no shame?" and then says that it is clear to them I am the cause of all of this. That I am a demon and that I am wreaking havoc and that I have one hour to leave before they set fire to my post. If I refuse to leave, they will come for me, all of them as a group.

She says all this very quickly, and they return down the hill. In my shock, I remain motionless until I feel the wetness in my trousers and realize that I have pissed myself. The daughter steps out, yawning, then looks curiously down at the three settlers marching toward a group of older gentlemen who are the council and who have gathered by the tree.

"It's nothing," I say, and smile. "Come. I want to show you something. I learned it from the missionary. We haven't seen him in a while, yes?"

The daughter eyes my trousers, then yawns once more and nods. I retrieve my teacup where there is a little honey left, and I walk toward the perimeter of the woods and hold it up. I hear her coming up behind me, the slow rustle of her skirt in the grass, but I don't turn.

A few minutes later, a bee appears, hovering, circling, then dips into the cup. Then it flies away into the woods. I follow it. She follows me. When I can't see it anymore or hear it anymore, I stand still and hold up the cup and wait for the bee to come back. Which it does. So we move on, and as we head farther into the woods, I tell the daughter that it is a trick I learned from the missionary. We're creating a trail.

"To the hive," I say. "And the honey."

And then I hold the cup out for her to try. Without hesitation she lifts it up, and after the bee leaves the cup, she begins to walk steadily and purposefully. She doesn't notice that I have stopped and that I am watching her.

The sun has entered the forest and the spaces between the trunks are alight. It is as if the trees vibrate. For a moment, there is no sound. And I know it is a trick of the light, but the farther away she goes, holding the cup in front of her, the taller she becomes. Not once does she turn. Her shoulders widen. Her hair grows long and pale. And then I hear a distant scream coming from behind me and I say out loud, "So it really isn't you."

I wonder if the hour has already passed. Whether they are all climbing the hill to burn down my post.

I try to imagine where you are now, Father. And where I should be. Why someone will refuse to leave a cursed place.

She is in the distance now. All sunlight. Only a sliver. The bee comes back from its hidden kingdom, and then it doesn't.

Your ever faithful nephew,
Andrei Bulavin

PERSON OF KOREA

He waits three weeks for his father to respond. During that time, whenever he checks the mail for a reply, the dog follows him. She eyes the birds on the telephone wires. Then the migrant workers in the fields.

One day, the pay phone near the mailboxes rings. He hurries to the booth. But it is a woman from Vladivostok conducting a survey of the Korean communities in the Russian Far East. The surveyors have been calling ever since Russia's first president was elected. He usually hangs up, but today he doesn't. The dog lies down beside him as he answers all of the surveyor's questions.

No, I don't work on the barley farm. No, we rent the house.

Yes, the electricity goes out often. Yes, the water tastes tinny. Yes, we have a store for basic groceries, but the nearest town is an hour south.

Yes, he lies. *I go to school.*

No, I don't use the pay phone often.

"Why?" the surveyor asks.

"Because you have to pay."

He hears her writing. Listening to her voice, he tries to remember the voice of his father.

"What's your name?" the surveyor asks.

"Maksim."

"How old are you?"

"Sixteen."

"How many people are in your household, Maksim?"

Maksim begins to count the people who live in the row of houses next to the farm until he realizes the woman is referring only to his family.

Maksim says, "Two in our household," knowing that is no longer true.

When he hangs up, the noise startles the dog awake. The dog follows Maksim back to the house, and once he is safely inside, she bolts into the field toward the far woods. She is no one's dog, but for the past few weeks she has followed only him. He leaves the door open for her. His uncle would never have allowed that, but his uncle is three weeks dead so what does it matter now.

Maksim is like the dog. He does what he wants. He wears what he wants to wear and eats when he wants to eat. He doesn't make up the mattress on the floor, and it doesn't matter if he knocks over a glass, startling himself awake from a dream he keeps having in which people are speaking to him in different languages he has never heard before. There is no one to explain the dream or to chastise him or to tell him to go to the corner store and see if there is work so that he can earn some money for the house.

There are only his uncle's things everywhere: his baseball cap on the wall hook, his tin mug and his stack of car magazines in this one-room house Maksim has lived in for longer than his father has been away. There is the door always swinging now from the wind that comes at the end of summer, and outside the barley that hasn't had rain in a long time, long enough for Maksim to know that it has been a bad year; a bad year after several, and there is talk of the migrant workers not returning.

Through the doorframe, he can still see the tire tracks of his uncle's taxicab. The company came the other day and towed it. As his neighbors watched, the truck driver tossed a road map to Maksim and told him it had been in the taxi's glove compartment. Maksim waited until he was alone before opening the map, wondering if by chance something else was folded in it, some secret message for him. But it was only a map, one his uncle hardly ever used because he knew the roads.

In the mailbox yesterday was a letter telling Maksim that his uncle owes money for the cab. Next month, Maksim will owe rent for the house. For the fourth time this week, he heads out to the corner store to ask the owner if he can do anything today. The owner ignores him and opens boxes of instant ramen as the newscaster on the television reports on a skirmish on the border to Chechnya.

Then the man tosses Maksim a ramen pack and says, "Why do you all keep eating only this shit?"

Later, Maksim opens the map again, but Chechnya isn't there. Sakhalin Island is there. East of where he is, next to the Sea of Japan. It is 950 kilometers long and 160 kilometers wide. It is like a giant, leaping fish. He draws a route from the mainland coast to the island coast, 100 kilometers back and forth, he reckons, and then spots a town called Terney on the mainland that he can get to in a few hours.

Maksim doesn't know if his father still works on Sakhalin or if he got the letter telling him that his brother, Maksim's uncle, is dead. He doesn't know what his father's favorite food is anymore. Whether he is fat or thin or speaks in Russian or Korean most days.

Maksim's father left for the island five years ago. Or was told to leave. Maksim has not seen him since.

The wind blows in. He cooks the ramen in the microwave, staring at the calendar marked up with his uncle's handwriting, unable to decipher it. It is the last day of August.

The month ends. The mailbox stays empty. Two days later, shutting the door behind him, Maksim walks to where the migrant workers are climbing onto the bed of a pickup truck and asks whether he can catch a ride with them. The workers are Koreans from Uzbekistan, and they have been coming here for years. They are heading east, he knows, to another farm, before they head south for the winter.

Maksim is standing on the road with a backpack on his shoulders. He is wearing a denim jacket and his uncle's baseball cap. Maksim holds out some money he had been keeping under his mattress, but the Uzbek closest to him says to keep it. In Korean, the Uzbek says they were sorry to hear about Maksim's uncle, that the man used to give them free rides. Then the workers help Maksim up and ask where he wants to go.

"Terney," he says.

As the truck begins to move, the dog leaps up onto the bed. The Uzbeks laugh. The dog looks up again at the birds on the wires as they all leave the farm.

•

"Your father still on the island?" The Uzbek beside him is shouting over the wind. They are speeding through a forest with a high canopy. "Is he still at the camp?"

Maksim isn't sure what they think of his father, so he just nods, holding the dog as the truck shakes.

Maksim's father is a prison guard. Or the last time they spoke he was, working at the prison on the island. The older people call it the camp because it was a labor camp run by the Japanese, when the Japanese claimed the southern half of the island. They rounded up thousands of Koreans during wartime and brought them there to log, pulp paper, mine coal. Maksim's grandfather, who was in his twenties, had been one of the laborers. When the war ended, many of them, including Maksim's grandfather, never went back home. They took a boat west, first to Vladivostok, then eventually headed inland, north, where they settled, had children, gave those children Russian names.

That is their family story. That is the story of almost all the families who rent on that farm.

He has always been aware of the strangeness of his father going to work where his own father was imprisoned. He once asked his uncle about it, but his uncle only said, "Better your father there than here," and left it at that.

They ride the rest of the way in silence. The forest turns into meadows and then into hills and dunes. Then, suddenly, the sea smell. Seabirds. When they pull into Terney, the Uzbek he was talking to hands him a piece of paper with an address near Vladivostok. He tells Maksim that they aren't sure there will be work at the farm next year—and that if things don't work out for Maksim, to come to them.

"We will see each other again," the Uzbek says.

The dog leaps down, following Maksim. Together they enter the hill town, heading directly to the coast. The afternoon air is sandy and cold and full of a heavy sound he doesn't yet realize is the movement of water. He has been on the road for over two hours and already he feels a world away. He grips the straps of the backpack and feels a rush of relief that the dog is here. He ducks under clotheslines. The dog steals some water from a bucket. Other dogs eye her, then vanish into alleys. He avoids looking at the windows.

It occurs to Maksim that he doesn't know the route his father took to the island. For many years now, he has imagined him in a guard uniform gripping a club and has wondered how the club has changed the way he strikes men. As a child, Maksim's greatest fear was that his father would one day use a kitchen knife.

He finds a path to the beach. The dog is elated. She bounds into the water and back as Maksim walks on the sand, listening, watching. He comes upon some wooden houses, a restaurant, and then a garage in which surfboards lie stacked on a rack. He returns to the restaurant. A gray-haired woman stands behind the bar, wiping the counter. Her eyes have a steadiness that makes him feel at ease, and so he asks, in Russian, whether she knows of anyone with a boat. She considers him and then points out toward the cliff and says that if he keeps going, he'll find the fishermen.

So he keeps going. He walks past some large rocks sticking up out of the water like miniature islands. When he reaches the base of the cliff, he spots the motorboats pulled up on the beach. In the shadow of the cliff is a cluster of shacks. Here the ocean sound is louder and everywhere. If someone were behind him, he wouldn't know. He turns. When he turns again, a group of people are approaching him from the shacks.

"That your dog?"

"She's no one's dog," Maksim says.

"Then I guess we can take her," a man says.

Maksim is silent. The dog stands rigid and is also silent. A woman is standing behind the group of men, smoking a cigarette, looking bored. Maksim asks if these are their boats. When the men don't respond, Maksim asks if they could take him to Sakhalin.

"I can pay," Maksim says.

Another man asks if he is Japanese—that the Japanese keep coming here with their surfboards and Jet Skis. We don't want your Japanese money, they say. But then a moment later they say, "Prove you've got the money." They inch closer, staring at him. One of them leans forward and claps his hands once, loudly.

The dog snarls. Maksim quickly turns and hurries away. He

counts to thirty. For every number he takes a step. Twenty-eight, step . . . twenty-nine, step. . . . He spins around, his hands clenched, but the group hasn't moved from where they were. They've lost interest in him.

Now he is alone. He and the dog. He approaches the large rocks he passed and begins to walk out into the water. From the shore, the dog watches. The rocks are slippery, but Maksim keeps going, treading carefully. He goes as far as he can without the waves splashing all over him and squints out into the vast nothing, searching for the island or even Japan.

Maybe he will try heading farther down the beach in the opposite direction and ask someone else. Or maybe he will try another town on the coast. He thinks of his uncle trying to teach him to swim one year but can't remember which beach they were on. Only that his uncle ended up swimming on his own and Maksim stayed on the sand, following him.

He thinks of moving here. Working at a restaurant. Finding a large piece of driftwood or a heavy rock and beating those fishermen one at a time, the others tied up and forced to watch.

He smiles. He hops back toward the sand where the dog is waiting, wagging her tail. Otherwise, the beach is empty. Stars are now visible and the sunset water is thick and undulating. He feels the strange pull of it. He asks the dog, "What next?"

He finds himself back at the restaurant. He steps onto the deck and peers in. The glass doors are locked, the lights off, and no one is inside. He sits on the steps facing the water and reaches inside his jacket pocket. He pulls out a pack of cigarettes that belonged to his uncle and smokes one. It helps his hunger. Then he realizes he has not fed the dog, has brought nothing for the dog. What a stupid thing to forget. He opens up his backpack as though food might magically appear. By now, the dog has fallen asleep, and Maksim tucks his feet under her body to keep warm.

He matches his breathing with the dog's. His eyes begin to close; the ocean comes and moves over him.

He jerks awake to someone lifting the brim of his baseball cap. The woman from the bar is leaning down. He has no idea what time it is—late enough that the water is lit by the night. He can see her there in the silver light. Then he wonders why the dog didn't bark, and turns.

"Where's my dog?"

"No dog," the woman says. "Did you find your boat?"

He shakes his head. He searches around him for tracks in the sand.

"You could try looking for a boat again in two days."

"Two days?"

"Rain tomorrow. Fog. Not good to see the sights, yes?"

"I'm not seeing the sights," Maksim says, and gets up.

Again, she considers him. "Come on," she says.

He says he needs to look for the dog, but she says, "The dog will come back."

She brings him inside the restaurant to the bar. She hands him a blanket and a glass of water and brings out a bowl for the dog, which she leaves outside. He asks if she has any food for the dog. She takes out a jar full of pretzels and peanuts.

"That's for you both," she says.

He twists open the gray lid and eats fistfuls of the snack. The salt wakes him. He drinks more water. She opens two beers and gives him one. He drinks it fast enough that it goes to his head. She sips hers and watches the television. Yeltsin is talking about Chechnya again. She glances at him, presses mute, and switches the channel to a soccer game.

"I'm Sofia," she says.

"Maksim."

"How old are you, Maksim?"

He lies. "Eighteen. You?"

She chuckles. She tells Maksim it was her husband's restaurant but doesn't go on.

"I wouldn't mind working at a restaurant," Maksim says.

"You might," Sofia says, and taps her fingernails against her beer.

He walks to the deck, looking for the dog. For the first time, Sofia asks what he is doing here, and he explains. He takes out the money too.

Sofia counts the money, returns it to him, and then says, "I know someone with a boat."

"You didn't say that earlier," Maksim says.

"I didn't know you earlier," Sofia says.

He tries to give her the money again but she refuses. On the television, a goalie dives and catches the ball. Sofia tells him to get some sleep, that she will see him tomorrow, and she turns the lights off and steps out.

Maksim lies down against the bar. The floor is sticky and smells of old beer. But a tiredness that is much greater than the trip today settles inside him. He concentrates on the ocean swell, thinking again of his uncle in the water.

•

The dog does not come back the next day. Sofia arrives in the morning and brings him to an old, tiny fishing trawler on the dock. She says it is her nephew's boat, and that she will take him herself. He hasn't told her that he has never been on a boat before.

A thick curtain of fog has settled on the coast. The air sticks to him. Soon they are off, pushing away from land and heading east into the Sea of Japan, into a fog that grows denser the farther they go. He sits on the floor beside her, his knees to his chest and his eyes closed, waiting for the nausea that has hit him to pass.

The trip takes hours. He keeps his eyes closed. Then he grows used to the rhythm of the boat and the engine noise, and as the nausea recedes, he stands, peering over Sofia's shoulder. At first he cannot see the island because of the fog. Then glimpses of it appear, and he spots the port and the tall green hills near the water. The port is busier than he thought it would be. He can see fishermen on the dock and a cargo ship a little farther down, everything vanishing and then reappearing in the fog.

They find an empty space for her to dock quickly. She asks how long he needs.

He hasn't thought about that. But he feels a new energy as he picks up his backpack. His heart beats fast.

"I can't stay here," she says. "So I'll come back tomorrow at noon. And if you're not here tomorrow, I'm calling the police. Deal?"

He nods. He almost asks her to come. He jumps off and turns. "My dog," Maksim says.

"Yes," Sofia says. "I'll find the dog."

He tightens the straps of his backpack and hurries through the fog down the dock. Seabirds have flocked on the main street, eating crumbs in the middle of the road. Every time a car races out of the fog, the birds startle and scatter.

Maksim takes a trail up the hill. He knows from the old stories that the prison isn't far from the dock—that his grandfather and the others could always smell the ocean. Maksim imagines them taking this same trail. Moving through this same fog. He wants to reach high ground, above the fog. But the higher he goes, the less he can see.

A wind gusts over him. Rounding a bend, he stumbles upon two men kneeling beside a boulder. One of them is placing something into a duffel bag. He retreats, unsure if they have noticed him, but the language they are speaking to each other catches his ear. He has never heard it before. Then he hears the men calling him over.

In Russian, Maksim asks if they know where the prison is.

"You turning yourself in?" The man closest to him grins.

"My father," Maksim says. "He's a guard."

The man's grin doesn't break. He says the trail will end soon, at an intersection where three roads go three ways. "Take the far right," he says. "It'll get you there. But stay on the curb. People speed here."

Maksim thanks them. Before he goes, he asks what language they were speaking.

Instead of answering, the man says, "You are *Koryo-saram,* yes?"

Koryo-saram. Person of Korea.

"Yes," Maksim says.

"We were here long before you, my friend." The man keeps grinning. "So long," he says, and his companion lifts the duffel bag and they both take the trail down and vanish into the fog.

Maksim finds the three roads, takes the far right one. He keeps to the side as the man said, following an empty field that reminds him of the farm. Almost half an hour later, the prison appears: high walls, barbed wire, and a tower. By the main entrance stands a booth with a guard inside.

When the guard notices him, Maksim says his father's name. He says his father is also a guard and that he is looking for him and that it is important. He says if the guard doesn't believe him, he should ask around.

The guard puts down the magazine he has been reading and leans forward. "You're Vasily's boy?"

Maksim nods.

The man checks a clipboard and says Vasily's shift hasn't started yet. "He's home," the guard says. "Go there."

Maksim doesn't know where that is.

The guard hesitates, then says, "Walk back to the road. Take a right and keep walking until you reach a hill where a cluster of houses overlooks the prison. If it weren't for the fog, you'd see the houses from here. You're really Vasily's boy?"

Maksim doesn't answer. He has been on the island now for over an hour. He pictures Sofia's trawler well on its way back to the mainland. The more tired his legs grow, the more the fog is like an ocean and the land is floating on it.

He reaches the houses. They are well-built, with sturdy new roofs—the kind he would like to live in one day. He is wondering which one is his father's when, almost at once, Maksim spots him behind the window of the first one. Vasily then steps out the back, lights a cigarette, and turns toward the road.

"Maksim!"

They stand facing each other. Maksim's eyes do not leave his father as Vasily sits on the bench beside a picnic table in the backyard, facing the prison below, though it is barely visible right now.

Five years. All those days seem to collapse. He cannot remember a single one.

Maksim sits across from him on the other bench. From here, he can see the back of the house, where a woman is staring at them through the doorway. She is wearing a bathrobe, and when she steps out, his father tells her to go back inside. She doesn't listen. She is Vasily's age and has very long hair that she has washed and blow-dried. The cigarette smell around them mixes with the smell of her shampoo.

She says, "That your boy?" but Vasily doesn't respond. Maksim doesn't either. He is looking at his father, who is clean-shaven for the first time he can recall and wearing a pressed shirt.

"He doesn't look like you at all," the woman says.

"He's better-looking than I am," Vasily says.

"That's the truth."

"You staying for a bit?" his father says.

The woman leans toward Vasily's ear. "I don't want no boy," she says, and walks back inside, taking the shampoo smell with her.

"You hungry, you want a beer?" his father says. Then he says, "How old are you now?"

A wind pushes over them, bringing the fog, erasing his father for a moment.

"It's a nice house," Maksim says.

"It's a good job. A steady one. Like I told you."

"You've lived here the whole time?"

Vasily shakes his head: He used to live farther away in an apartment complex. The houses here were built by the new government. A lottery was set up for guards who were interested; he was one of the winners and moved here last year.

Maksim pictures his father winning a house. He tries to recall if they ever won anything. "That's some luck," Maksim says, and his father takes a drag of his cigarette, shutting one of his eyes so the smoke doesn't go in.

"I remember that hat," Vasily says.

Maksim takes off his uncle's baseball cap and places it on the tabletop.

"He knew nothing about baseball," his father says. "He just liked the hat."

"He knew a little," Maksim says.

His father looks down as though he is recalling something, then asks how the house is, who is living there these days on that farm road, and Maksim considers how to answer. He wants to say there have been bad years at the farm. The corner store isn't making enough money to hire him, and he can't pay next month's rent. He wants to say he isn't sure he will be there anymore and is thinking of going somewhere else, except he doesn't know where to go.

"Did you get the letter?" Maksim says.

"I did."

"You didn't come to the funeral."

"I didn't know if he would've wanted me there," Vasily says. "I didn't know if you would've either."

Maksim breaks away from his stare, turns to the hillside. He points down below. "Was any of that the camp?" he says.

"The what?"

"The labor camp. Grandad."

His father doesn't know.

"Do you think of him?" Maksim says. "When you're working in there? I would think of him all the time. If I was working there."

"Then I'm glad you aren't working there," Vasily says. After a pause, he softens his voice and says there's too much going on inside the prison to think of much.

"Do you know why Grandad ended up where he did?" Maksim says. "Why he stayed in this country?"

"Yeah," Vasily says. "He got on the wrong boat."

He can't tell if his father is joking. Then his father laughs. Maksim is startled. He can't remember the last time he heard his father laugh. It is like ash being thrown over a small fire inside him.

"Do you remember a dog?" Maksim says. "At the farm?"

"I've got no use for dogs," his father says.

"She's a Rhodesian Ridgeback. The breed came from Africa. The workers told me that. I caught a ride with them."

"What's Africa got to do with me. Or you."

"I'd like to go to Africa," Maksim says.

Vasily stubs out his cigarette. "You came all this way to ask if I got your letter, to talk about your grandfather, and to tell me you're going to Africa?"

"No," Maksim says. "I came to say two other things."

His father waits.

Maksim's throat tightens. He looks down and grips the edge of the tabletop. He says, "I don't know if you were planning on coming back to check on me. But if you were, I don't need you to."

"You don't need me to, yeah?" his father says.

"Yeah," Maksim says. "I'm okay. I'm okay on my own."

His father reaches across and Maksim flinches. His father laughs some more and then, to Maksim's surprise, he reaches across more carefully and takes Maksim's hand. He takes his hand gently as though they are praying together. Maksim fixes his gaze down at the fog slipping in under him. The way it floats there around his legs like something ancient and alien.

"Do you use a club?" Maksim says.

He says it quietly, but Vasily hears.

"What?"

"At the prison. Do you use a club?"

He feels the pressure of his father's hand against his own. He waits for the break in the silence, for his breath to be knocked away, for that sudden crack in the world, and it is like he wants it to happen. He doesn't understand why he would want that. It is like the way the dog bounds across the barley fields into the woods as though being drawn there by something the dog can't control.

But nothing happens. His father does nothing. He lets go of Maksim's hand, and the wanting vanishes as quickly as it came. All of a sudden, the air fills with a foreign noise. A siren. An alarm. It fills this corner of the island. Maksim thinks perhaps it is an airplane, but then bright lights flicker down below at the prison.

From inside the house the telephone rings, and the woman appears, waving the receiver.

His father goes inside. He comes back out a few minutes later, buttoning up his uniform.

"Someone broke out," he says. "It's all right. It's nothing to worry about. It happens a few times a year."

Maksim watches as, below, a pickup truck comes out of the prison and approaches the house.

"You know who it is?" Vasily says. "It's always those Nivkhs. They break the law and get punished for it and they think they can just walk out. Because they think it's their island and they can do whatever they want. We try, you know? We try to be good to them. We even hire some as guards. Then all they do is break one of their friends out."

Maksim has stopped listening to his father. He is thinking of the two men he ran into on the trail. The duffel bag. One of the men grinning at him. The cadence of their language. Nivkh.

The truck pulls up out front. Maksim walks around with his father. Vasily goes on: "Do you know? All they ever do is go home. The world changes, it will always change, and they will always stay the same. Why do you think that is? Stubborn fools."

Before Maksim can say anything back, his father says: "Maksim, what was the second thing?"

"The second thing?"

"That you wanted to say to me," his father says. "You said you came to say two things. What is the second thing?"

Two guards with rifles are in the cab, staring at Maksim.

"Is there anyone else?" Maksim says.

"Anyone else?"

"In our family," Maksim says. "Is there anyone else, somewhere else?"

"Hell if I know," Vasily says, and jumps onto the bed of the pickup.

The truck speeds away. The woman is now by the front door, but Maksim ignores her. He feels a lingering heat where his father held his hand, focused there in his palm. He keeps feeling it as he passes the prison and gets back on the trail. At the port, he searches for Sofia's trawler, in case she never left. Some fishermen are staring up over the hills at the noise.

It is then that he realizes he forgot his uncle's baseball cap on the picnic table. For a moment, the air goes quiet. He sees nothing in the fog but panning light—the dog in the field; his uncle swimming. He reaches out. Then a car rushes by, swift and dark, almost touching him as the alarm continues to sound, louder now, across the island.

VALLEY OF
THE MOON

Two years later, he left the settlement.

He took the bus heading north and then hitchhiked on the back of a repurposed US Army truck that was filled with others like him who all said the same thing: they were heading home.

They all said this knowing that there wasn't much left for them to go to. Still, it felt good to say this to each other, to say without saying that they had survived, and as the truck made stops, they exchanged cartons of cigarettes, small sacks of grain, shoelaces, pieces of cloth. Then they asked each other where home was and how far from the border they would be living. They asked what refugee settlement the others had found themselves in or how many and for how long or if they had been in one at all. They asked each other what they had done before the war, and they asked each other their names and how old they were.

His name was Tongsu. He was like so many of them from a farming family and he was thirty-one years old.

Crowded together in the back of the bumpy truck, they asked him about his eye patch. He was honest and told them that when he'd first arrived at the settlement, he had been stabbed during a scuffle. Some of them showed him the toes or the fingers they were missing from frostbite during winter. Tongsu did the same—he was missing a small toe—and then they made a joke about how maybe what they had lost would turn up now that the war was over.

"Tongsu, I will remember you!" they all said, when it was his turn to get off the bus, and he said that he would remember them too, knowing he wouldn't.

When he reached the mountains, he walked. He walked the road until he reached a part that had been bombed out and then he walked into the woods and climbed the steep slope. A large sack of rice grains was strapped to his back with the moth-bitten wool blanket he had used for sleeping. Hidden in the grains was a large amount of money he had taken from the inside wall of the shanty where he and a dozen others slept, money that had belonged to a man who had died a year earlier. In Tongsu's chest pocket, tucked inside a handkerchief, were vegetable seeds.

He climbed steadily without rest, using the trees that had survived to pull himself up. He climbed for almost an hour, zigzagging up the slope. When he eventually reached the crest, he could see below, almost halfway down the other side, the small farmhouse where he had been born and where his parents had most likely died, he didn't know. It was more than half in ruin, as was most of the land, the soil upturned and dried out. Deep craters were everywhere. Pieces of rubber and metal. He spotted the bones of animals, some of them likely belonging to the goats that used to roam here, and he wasn't sure why but he spent the rest of the day gathering them, the bones, even before he stepped inside.

When he did, it had grown dark, only the moonlight to guide him through this house he had not seen in a lifetime, where in the one room that remained intact he found only a cup on the floor brimming with old dirt and rainfall.

•

Tongsu spent a year fixing up the house. He found thatch to repair the roof and wood to build a fence for the eventual animals he planned to have. He planted new grass. Once a month, he walked the four hours into the nearest village and purchased supplies he needed or, once the vegetables and rice began to grow, used food to barter with. Every season, a tinker passed through the valley, and Tongsu was able to get from the man cookware, pots, more cups. It turned out the tinker recognized him from when he was a boy, but as hard as Tongsu tried to remember the old man, he couldn't.

"It's good to see someone again," the tinker said. "In the Valley of the Moon."

Tongsu had forgotten people called it that. He asked if there was anyone else around here—he recalled another farm farther down the valley, around a bend—but the tinker shook his head. "Who wants to live out here? Only you. Not even the soldiers guarding the border about a day's journey north want to be there." The tinker laughed. Then he slapped the mule and said, "At least they buy my stuff," and sang a song loud enough that it kept echoing back as he grew smaller and smaller in the distance.

Other than the tinker or a village person, Tongsu saw no one else. This became his life. He grew his own food. He repaired the roof when it leaked and caught rabbits and eventually found someone from whom he could purchase a goat. He began to think less of that time when he had lived surrounded by voices and yelling and crying and praying and noises he had never heard before; and bodies sleeping and living and shitting and pissing and working around him.

Here, he woke and slept to complete silence. Not even a plane. Sometimes the sound of an engine—a car or a tank—but that was rare. Only on occasion the clanking of the tinker's wagon passing somewhere through the valley. He kept track of the growing grass. The return of birds. He grew a long beard then cut it and then grew it again. One summer, he got a record player with a faded sticker of an army base—how did it get to the village?—and a stack of records and listened to music.

Sometimes at the start of evening, he would pack a bottle of wine and walk all the way down the valley. Hearing his music playing faintly but clearly, he found the cluster of large, pale stones scattered along the valley floor that was not from the war but from long before.

Every night, the moon rose from here, and fell, and shattered. And then built itself back up again.

He remembered that from when he was a child. He had never liked the story—had avoided this area as a child. It had frightened him, but he was too embarrassed to say that out loud. He realized he didn't often think of his parents and his sister anymore, but with the wine in him and sitting on one of the pale, large stones, he did down there. Strangely, or at least he thought so, what came to him most vividly were their hands, or the feel of their hands, and the sweet, sweat smell of his sister's hair. But he could recall neither their faces nor their voices anymore. He thought if he saw them, say in a dream, or as ghosts, he would. But he never dreamed of them. And their ghosts had yet to visit him.

Which was what he thought was happening one night when he opened his eyes to find someone crouched across from him on another stone. Tongsu had been living on the farm for a few years now. He had drunk too much wine and fallen asleep. The record player in his house high above was skipping, a precise repetition like heartbeats. Slowly Tongsu sat up, worried that if he moved too quickly the vision would go away. He was startled, holding his breath, but he was not afraid.

The ghost was avoiding the moonlight. And then it spoke: "I was told to come find you."

"Me?" Tongsu said.

"I need to get across."

It was a man's voice. In that moment, Tongsu realized the man across from him wasn't a ghost at all. The man lifted a finger, piercing the moonlight like a knife.

"What happened to your eye?" he said.

When Tongsu didn't answer, the man went on: "I've got the money. Please. I need to get across."

The man threw a canvas bag at his feet. It hit the empty wine bottle with a thud.

"I think you have me mixed up with someone else," Tongsu said, growing more sober as his mind raced to gauge the situation he had found himself in. His tongue felt heavy. Not because of the wine but because he had not talked to anyone in months. When the man stood and jumped over to his rock, Tongsu was so shocked by the sudden enormity of the silhouette, the stranger's proximity, that it took him a moment to feel the hand grabbing his shoulder and then the pistol that was digging into his rib. It felt like a veil had been thrown over Tongsu so that everything that seemed to be happening was briefly delayed.

"Please," the man said. "I need to get across." The man mentioned a family he had not seen in years. How they had been separated and how he had lost track of them. How he couldn't even remember their faces. "Can you even imagine what that's like?" he shouted. He threw Tongsu off the rock and jumped on him and began to strike him. Tongsu covered his face, each strong blow hitting his wrist. His eye patch fell off. In that moment, he reached out desperately, grabbed a stone, and swung, landing a direct hit against the side of the man's head.

Tongsu was on top of the man now and that was when the pistol went off. It was quieter than he thought it would be. Like a soft balloon popping. He thought at first he had been shot, he felt the warmth and the wet all over him, but when he looked down it wasn't his blood. The man's eyes widened. Tongsu kicked himself away and the two of them faced each other once again, leaning against separate rocks.

"I just wanted to get across," the man said, and hiccupped.

Tongsu looked down. He was holding the pistol now. He aimed it at the man's chest, and when the man hiccupped again, Tongsu squeezed the trigger. And then it was quiet again, just the record, in the distance, continuing to skip.

•

Tongsu stayed there across from him all night. He waited in case the man was still alive, and he waited to see if anyone else was coming. He listened. He faced his house to see if he could spot anyone there. He tried to remember if the shot was loud enough for the soldiers a day away to hear, and then couldn't remember if a sound could travel that far.

At the refugee settlement, they could hear bombs halfway across the country. There was a time when in a late-night insanity he thought all sounds could travel far across the country, even his own breathing—especially his own breathing—so that what he had to do was stop his own breathing.

He never did that again. He breathed now. He breathed and waited. The sun came up. The valley around him clarified. The rocks grew more brown and the field green and the trees everywhere showed the start of fall. He was unaware of how cold he was until he tried to move. His whole body felt broken. The pistol felt glued to his palm. His eye patch was by the canvas bag and he reached for it, slipping it back on.

Then he opened the bag for the first time and saw the money and closed the bag again.

In the morning light, he could see the man now. He was older than Tongsu, perhaps in his late forties, and pencil thin, and had a beard. The blood had thickened almost to a paste and covered his entire front as if someone had emptied a can of paint on him. The man's eyes were open. The shine of them had left, the way it always did in the dead, so that the eyes did not seem real. The wounds were already attracting flies.

Tongsu's first thought was to walk to the soldiers. Or the town. Then he concluded that they would be suspicious of him and would never believe the story. Someone would ask why the man thought Tongsu could take him across.

He thought of all the routes and the avenues that led to tomorrow and another tomorrow and another one. The day grew brighter. A wind came. Still no one. If the tinker was close, he would hear the clank of his wagon first.

Tongsu forced himself up. He dropped the pistol and picked up the bag and headed as fast as possible to his house.

The record was still spinning, the needle scratching the center. He left it on and drank a glass of water. He hung the bag on a nail by the front door but changed his mind and took the money out and hid it in a ceramic pot. Then he took out a hoe and a shovel and climbed back down.

He almost believed the body wouldn't be there. He almost wished it wasn't.

But of course the body was there. Tongsu looked around one more time, listening, and began to dig beside the stones. He worked through the morning, and then he buried the pistol, the man, the empty canvas bag, and even the wine bottle.

And then Tongsu walked back up, collapsed on the floor, and slept.

He expected someone would eventually come looking for the man. He thought about this every day, waited for this every day. The more he thought about it, the more the days kept to how they were before the man appeared. A month went by. And then another. In the evenings, he walked down to where he had buried the man. Drinking wine, Tongsu talked to him.

He said, "Is there anyone coming? No? Why not? Because they are all on the other side? That's a pity."

He said, "Now we're friends. Find my parents instead. They will take care of you now."

He said, "Thank you for your money. I will buy animals with it."

He bought another goat as well as chickens and a pig. The pig followed him around all through the house and he let it sleep with him on the mat on the floor and sometimes he woke to find his arm wrapped around the contented animal. He stopped talking to the buried man but talked to the animals instead.

He bought a new eye patch from the tinker who didn't have any but made him one on the spot using cloth from a military uniform. He asked the tinker for any news from the border, but the tinker shrugged. He said instead that a church van was driving around the mountains, not too far from here, wondering if people needed help in their homes—taking care of them, rebuilding them.

When Tongsu slipped one day after a day of rain, twisting his ankle badly enough that he knew he couldn't work for a few days, he thought of the church van.

When he was well enough, Tongsu walked to the village. He had made a walking stick and it helped, but it was a four-hour walk and the pain had returned by the time he made it to the village. He found the scribe who wrote letters for people and asked if the church van had passed through yet. When the scribe shook his head, Tongsu asked if he could leave a message for them.

A week later, Tongsu heard movement on the slope behind him and walked out to find two kids, a boy and a girl, brushing dirt off their trousers. They said they were from the church and that they would be happy to work for him if he needed it. The girl was named Eunhae and she was eleven; the boy, Unsik, was ten.

Tongsu asked if they were orphans and the girl said, "We wouldn't be part of that stupid church if we weren't."

This made him laugh. He liked her. He told them what to do, and he fed them, and in the evening he rolled out the moth-bitten wool blanket for them on the floor to sleep on; he built a fire and told them to sleep beside it for warmth.

The next morning, he thought he would wake to find them gone, but they were still there. And they were there at night and still there the following morning. Soon the kids were living on the farm, and it was only a matter of time before he unofficially adopted them or at least asked if that would be all right by them, and they nodded. He said they didn't have to call him their father, that he wasn't expecting them to. They didn't, but he noticed as the years went on that they called each other brother and sister.

Now he could send them into town together and not do it on his own. Some days they cooked, and they assigned birthdays for each other and also celebrated his own, though he never told them his age, told them to guess, it was more fun that way, and they guessed that he was much older than he really was, and they gave him gifts they made or ones they had gotten from the church people whom they spoke to on occasion using the landline that was installed.

The mountain roads were rebuilt. It was easier to access the house and the valley, but no one seemed interested in visiting. It was a forgotten place. That was what he thought. And he wondered if that bothered the children, he didn't know, they didn't talk about that. They walked with him at the start of evening to the stones across the valley floor, and it was the boy who one day noticed a small knife etching on one of the surfaces. Tongsu had done this absentmindedly during that year when he would walk down in the evenings, sit down, and talk.

Tongsu didn't know what to say. And then the not-knowing grew into a frustration that bloomed inside of him—not unlike those nights at the settlement when a man beside him would not stop talking or weeping or panting—and he grabbed Unsik's shirt collar and told him it had nothing to do with him, what did he know about things like that.

In the moonlight, the boy stiffened and looked first down the valley and then at Eunhae, who had brought her knees up to her chest. It was then, seeing the girl like that, that Tongsu released his grip, cleared his throat, and ruffled the boy's hair. Then he tapped Eunhae lightly on her knee and leaned forward and told them both that his wife was buried here.

He said, in the chaos of the war, you buried people where you could. He said he was lucky she could be buried here at home.

That was the first time he had lied to them and the last time he ever would.

"Would you like to be buried here?" Unsik said, looking back at him now. "When you are gone?"

Eunhae flicked him and said that he was continuing to be disrespectful. But Tongsu waved a hand in the air and took some time that evening thinking about it.

"Yes," he said.

•

One day not long after that conversation, while feeding the animals, Tongsu felt a shadow pass over him. In the valley, Unsik was leading a man toward the house. Tongsu watched as they navigated the stones and began to climb the slope.

He told Eunhae, who was beside him, to go inside and not come out until the man was gone. He said this in a tone the girl had never heard before, much different from when he had yelled at her brother—this time both urgent and controlled—and so she did as she was told, sliding closed the door and pulling down the shutters.

Tongsu took out his knife, checked the blade, and slipped it behind him under his waistband.

Even from a distance, Tongsu knew the man was not from here. He was wearing country clothes that were clearly new, clothes that seemed meant for taking long treks but had never been worn—the shirt too crisp, the wool vest too bright, the boots clean of any scuff marks. And then, closer, the hair that had clearly been a government haircut but was growing out. But which government, the North or the South?

When the stranger made it to the house, he wiped his brow with his handkerchief, looked down to where he had climbed, and said, "Time never reached here. If I wanted to hide, it would be here. What beautiful country."

Tongsu told him he wasn't hiding, and the man wiped his brow again and grinned. Unsik noticed the door and the windows closed, and when Tongsu told him to go inside, the boy bowed. The man thanked Unsik for leading him all the way here from the village and offered him some coins. Unsik took them and hurried inside.

Then the stranger bowed and said to please forgive him, but he was looking for an uncle who had vanished some years ago and was last seen in these mountains.

"There are a lot of mountains," Tongsu said.

"Yes," the stranger said. "Quite."

The stranger walked over to the animals and inspected them. "He never came home," he said. "This would have been three years after the war. He would have come this way."

Tongsu asked the stranger where he was from, but the man didn't respond. He went on: "He would have climbed up and passed through this ridge to enter the valley. Because the roads were a mess back then. You remember. Craters from bombs and from shelling everywhere. I'm sure you know this, but they used to bury animals and the un-claimed dead in them and then if those holes weren't full enough, they would use whatever else they could—sacks of stones, tin drums, wood—so that vehicles could cross. Transport vehicles all over the country, carrying supplies, tires, concrete, animals. A pig passing over the bones of another one. Isn't that something? That was reconstruc-tion back then. But you know that too. Which camp did you spend the war in? Were you in Busan? One of the shantytown settlements? Did you ever need to find someone you had lost? You went to the forty steps there, didn't you. That was where you went to find someone in Busan. Everyone knew that. On those steps near the port, you could listen to an accordion player playing a song or buy popcorn from a street vendor and find your person. You're lucky, you know. You were displaced, but safe. Maybe not from each other and your petty greed and insignificant dramas, but from the greater madness. I would will-ingly be displaced for my entire life just to be safe from that. Not my uncle. He survived the war only for it to take him later when it was all over. What happened to your eye?"

Tongsu, who had reached behind him for his knife as he listened to the stranger, wondering if he could move faster than this man— and where he would position himself to make sure the stranger didn't enter the house—asked what he meant by the war taking his uncle after it was over.

The stranger paused. He was pretending badly to not notice the hand Tongsu had behind his back. Then he bowed again and asked for Tongsu's forgiveness. He said he was tired from the long walk and from the years of looking for his uncle. He asked if Tongsu would be hospitable enough to offer him a glass of water. Tongsu took his own cup and walked it over to the pump. The man gulped the water down and wiped his mouth with his handkerchief. Then he bowed a third time and offered the cup back with both of his hands.

"I was sorry to hear about your wife," the man said.

Tongsu wasn't sure if his face revealed anything, but the man said the boy had mentioned the grave down there. "The moon rises," the man said, "and falls and shatters. And then it builds itself back up again."

He bowed a fourth time, not as deep, and then without saying anything else, not even a good-bye, the man walked around the house and over the ridge into the forest that would lead him down the other side of the mountain.

•

Although Tongsu never saw the stranger again, and no one else came asking about a missing person, the strangeness of the encounter and the unsettledness of it hummed inside his chest for the remaining years of his life. It was at first like a fly that was trapped around his heart, something he learned to ignore, only for it to turn later on, as he grew older, into a claw.

There were times when he avoided walking down the valley altogether or refused to leave the house. He sat looking out, or paced the grounds, and he let the kids who were no longer kids do everything around the house. He ignored their glances and ate what they made him and went out again to sit and stare across at the valley floor.

There were also periods in his life when the feeling went away, when it seemed he could reclaim the days, only for the face of the stranger or the stranger's voice to return in a dream where Tongsu kept tripping over the bones of animals and could never climb out of the crater he had found himself in, a silhouette high above him peering down.

Perhaps this was the cause of Tongsu hitting Unsik one day when a pig died. Or perhaps it was the grief of the pig dying that caused him to behave illogically and recklessly and selfishly. He found the pig, which had apparently died peacefully in its sleep on the grass, and he went straight for Unsik. Tongsu struck him and pushed him against the side of the house, closed his fist, and punched him. Unsik, staggering, opened his eyes, his face filling all at once with shock and confusion. Unsik reached out with both hands, as though trying to hold up a wall that was about to topple over, and that was when Tongsu punched him again, and then kept punching him until Unsik's nose split open. Tongsu did all this silently, forgetting whom he was hitting, his vision gone black, unaware of Eunhae screaming behind him and clawing at his back so hard that she ripped his shirt, her nails digging into him and causing his skin to form rivers.

Eunhae was by then seventeen, a young woman, and that night she caught Tongsu looking at her for a beat longer than he normally did, caught him in the wake of whatever storm had erupted inside of him that day. She had buried the pig by herself and was across the room, caring for her brother, using a warm, damp cloth to wipe his face that was no longer recognizable, a lock of her hair falling over her own face. And as she tucked her hair behind her ear, she felt Tongsu's eyes on her—the foreign heat of him from across the room, like a drowsy, ancient bear who had lived many lives and was now weary and impatient in the back of a cave, watching.

The siblings left not too long after. Not together. Unsik, who lost partial vision in one of his eyes, sneaked away one night before it grew light. Instead of a note, Unsik left Eunhae a piece of paper he had folded into an origami boat—the tinker had taught him this, and Unsik, when he first saw, thought it was magic—and the socks she was always stealing from him.

They would never see each other again. She would never know of his many lives, not without adventure, first on the southern coast as a dockworker, and then on the island of Jeju as a fisherman, where he would father a child with a married woman, which would force him to leave them both, the woman and the child, and hop on a ship en route to Hamburg, Germany. It was there that Unsik spent the rest of his days working in the port, operating a crane until the day he was killed with a broken bottle to his neck during a bar fight.

In all those years, he would never know his sister left the same day he did, left the one-eyed farmer and the house that had been their home, left the valley, walking first to the village, looking frantically for her brother, and then catching a ride with the scribe who was now retired and was going to visit a war memorial on the anniversary of the armistice. From there, she found another ride, and then another, somewhere the desire to find Unsik folding together with a new desire to keep moving, to keep moving, to keep moving.

A week later, she ended up in the small city of Daegu, where she would spend almost the entirety of her twenties and where the days would rush forward even faster than they had, leaping like a young animal. The church that had brought her up to the valley, which was based in that city, connected her with a pharmacy where she manned the register three days a week. She found a room to rent at an all-women boardinghouse near the river. She developed insomnia. Every night she climbed out onto the rooftop to smoke cigarettes and listen to a neighbor's radio that was always turned on too loud to an American GI station that only played rock 'n' roll. Looking at the river and the city, she understood slowly, and then quickly, that the country had been changing dramatically while they had lived in that "forgotten" valley, changing still, in ways she could see and in ways she couldn't.

One night, a woman from the boardinghouse asked her if she liked to dance. Eunhae didn't know—she had never danced, not at the farm-house, not even with those records, or before those years. But she went with the woman anyway, avoiding the police as they held hands and hurried toward the outskirts of the city, to the basement of an abandoned factory where Eunhae froze under a brick arch, letting go of the woman's hand, confronted by a wall of sound—was that jazz?— and a forest of shadows: everyone inside ignoring the stink of sewage and flailing their arms, twisting their hips, jumping, dancing.

It was a space Eunhae would keep coming back to over the years, staying right up until curfew, wanting to be swallowed by the boom of music and a crowd, the momentary disorientation and claustrophobia that evolved into a sense of fullness and optimism.

She kept in touch with the church. On weekends she helped them host community dinners, and she drove the homeless around to receive medicine and vaccinations. She met old men and old women who had been born in the north but never returned after the border wall went up. She met people heading off to Germany to be nurses and miners for more money than they had ever made in all their lives, and she met American GIs at the base who were sometimes kind and other times cruel, obnoxious, and dumb. She met people who supported the new government and others who wanted to wage another war with them. She watched protests, fled protests, and then later watched a policeman line up a group of boys against a wall, take a pair of scissors from his belt, and trim their hair, which was an inch too long.

She saved money to take the bus around the city just to see what was being built and what had been abandoned and given up on. She fed as many of the strays as she could and she had conversations with university students who called themselves activists and intellectuals and musicians and painters and one day a hotel receptionist who thought she should come work for them, that she would meet all kinds of people from all over the country and sometimes from other countries. And that often they left things behind the staff could take, things like socks and chocolate. The woman winked when she said this.

By then, over a decade had passed since Eunhae had left the valley. And it was in the lobby of that hotel, working the night shift, that she turned twenty-eight. Because of the curfew, it was uneventful, but she loved being in the lobby, the pretty lights, the space that never smelled of sewage, the empty city visible through the lobby windows.

She learned to appreciate the quiet again. The nights. There was always a notepad to doodle on. A Japanese comic book a guest had left behind, Eunhae unable to read it but savoring the boxes of illustrations. The calendar that she would flip a few times until she reached the year 1980, a time that seemed impossibly foreign to her.

And almost every day, Eunhae was aware that she was living a life she could neither have conceived of nor made sense of two decades ago. Where was that girl now?

One late night at the hotel, not knowing exactly why, she picked up the phone and dialed the number she hadn't forgotten, the landline to the house in the valley, and when he picked up, she paused, listening to him breathing, his voice saying, "Hello, hello?" and she hung up.

A few days later, she called back, hung up, and then she called again, and again, not too often, perhaps once a month. Tongsu always picked up. He said, "Hello, hello?" and eventually she answered his hello, and they began to talk.

Which was how she got back in touch with the one-eyed farmer who had taken care of them. They talked two or three times a year, mostly near a holiday, or the farmer's birthday. They never talked about the past, or what had happened, or any memory they had of each other and of those years. They talked about the small things in the day—he had gotten some new chickens; the scribe had died; so had the tinker; she had finished a comic book she thought he might like.

Why?

Because it features a pig.

Silence. His breathing. There was a rumor that South Korea was planning on making a bid for one of the future Olympics, she said. She had heard that, but couldn't believe it. To think of the world coming here one day. The whole world. It almost made her laugh. She tapped her pen on the notepad. And then when he didn't respond, she told him something she wasn't supposed to tell anyone, a secret—but whom would he tell?

There were diplomats coming to stay at her hotel, she said. Important people she would have to greet. She was nervous about that. She didn't even know what a diplomat was.

"Pretend they're goats," he said.

"Goats?"

"That used to calm you. To see the goats on the mountain. When you were scared or crying from a nightmare, or missing your mother."

Eunhae had no memory of this. Just as she would have no memory of greeting the diplomats when they arrived or greeting some others the next year, when they stayed at the hotel again. She finished her shift and then she met some people at a house near the river. A jazz band was there. A piano and a trumpet that sang like slow-falling leaves.

She lost track of time. It grew late, almost past curfew. The buses had stopped coming. She thought she could walk it, and she did, the music trailing her as she followed the river, sensing something behind her, but trying to ignore it. When she turned, she saw two silhouettes in the near distance, walking her way.

There was no one else on the river road. The shops were closed. She caught a distant siren. She turned around again, and they were there, still following. She thought of running, intended to, but she froze. She would think of this sometimes, later, unable to remember how long she was on that road that night, stopped in the middle of it, her body unable to move as though waiting for the inevitable, wondering why it was a thing she was waiting for, wanting to scream but unable to as the two men hurried up behind her and then passed, a pocket of air, not even looking her way but deep in their own private conversation and holding hands briefly, she saw, before they parted, one continuing down the road, the other across a bridge, running now like her brother ran, long strides, stopping to turn once, believing she, Eunhae, from that distance was his lover, a silhouette that he waved to in reckless happiness as the clock struck midnight.

•

It wasn't long after this that Eunhae took a weekend off and caught a bus heading north. As she left the city, evidence of fall began to appear; the colors of the trees grew deeper and bolder. The woman beside her had an arm in a sling. When they were far enough out of the city, the woman slipped off the sling and began knitting. She knitted the whole way up, though what she was making Eunhae couldn't tell. Whenever the bus hit a bump, their elbows touched, but they never spoke. Eunhae got off first.

From the start of that mountain road, she walked. It was fully paved over now. She stayed to the side of it as a car or a truck raced by. A light rain began to fall. More like a mist. It was not unpleasant and went away before she got soaked. She wiped the beads of it away from her sweater and paused when she thought she heard a song playing, a humming, only to realize it was a bird.

There were no animals when Eunhae arrived at the cabin, not a single one. When no one answered, she walked in and saw him sitting beside his tea table with his legs crossed on the floor, leaning against the wall with his mouth open and his hand clutching his chest.

She didn't know how long he had been dead. She had not talked to him in months, but it appeared that he had died recently. There was a faint smell to him, and a fly buzzed away when she approached, but otherwise it was as though he had fallen asleep. Save for the hand on his chest—he had been clawing his skin, a heart attack?—he looked peaceful sitting there. His hair, which had turned all white, was combed neatly, the comb itself in his chest pocket, in front of his handkerchief.

The only thing odd to her was that he was not wearing his eye patch, and she wondered if he had stopped wearing it some time ago. It occurred to Eunhae that she had never seen him without it, not once. It occurred to her also that she didn't know how old he was exactly. He could not have been older than seventy.

She knelt and leaned forward to fully look at him. She kept waiting to feel afraid, but the fear never came. She tried to move his hand away from his chest, but his body had stiffened too much. She bumped against the tea table. The cup there was full of tea, and it spilled a little. She dipped her finger into the cup—cold—and almost put her finger into her mouth, but paused. She turned around and listened. Nothing. She looked at him again. The hand on his chest and the dark coin of skin where his eye had once been. She rubbed the tea between her fingers, sniffed, and wiped down her hands.

She searched the house, but it was as it always was. Perhaps not as clean or tidy—they did that, she and her brother—but the same otherwise. The record player was there; his walking stick; his mat rolled up as though there would be another evening and morning. The only thing missing was his eye patch, and she walked around again trying to find it, and then when she couldn't, she cleaned up a bit, taking away the teacup, pouring it out, and sat down again in front of him for a while.

From her pocket, Eunhae took out the origami boat her brother had left for her all those years ago. For the first time, she unfolded it, knowing there wasn't anything there but hoping anyway the way she used to, wanting every night on that rooftop overlooking the river when she couldn't sleep, listening to someone's rock 'n' roll, to take the origami boat apart but unable to. Now she flattened the empty paper across the tea table and left it there, thinking of what Tongsu had said to them both a long time ago.

She unplugged the telephone. She closed the windows and looked back at Tongsu one more time and went out to find a shovel and a hoe.

The sun was setting by the time Eunhae reached the stones at the bottom of the valley. She found the stone with the knife markings on it and then stepped a few paces to the side and began to dig. She dug and used her boot to sink the shovel in, and when she came upon some rocks she used the hoe.

It grew dark. Even in the cold, she was sweating. The moon came up, and when the shovel hit something that was not dirt or rock, she didn't hear or feel it at first. She had lifted the shovel, ready to strike again, when the moonlight shifted, and she stopped. She got on her knees. She brushed the dirt away and lifted up a large, heavy sack and unwound the twine.

Inside was a large collection of animal bones. She picked up what was probably a rib or a leg. And also, the skull of something small, perhaps a rabbit. Also, the skull of a goat. Hooves. She had no idea how old the bones were or whether it was even Tongsu who had buried them. Or whether it was a history much older than his or her own.

She sat down on one of the stones and thought of the multitude of animals that had lived and passed through here. The ones that were cared for, eaten, released, left behind, caught in gunfire and shelling, ran, were terrified into stillness, were born, lived, played with each other, breathed.

Her body hurt. Eunhae wondered if she should go on with the digging. Whether it was silly and irresponsible, what she was doing.

She wished Unsik were here. She wondered where he was. What he looked like these days. Whether he was alone or with someone right now. Whether she would wake one day and sense that he was gone. Or whether he had already gone.

She thought about how a decision could reveal all the different layers of life, which felt to her as unreachable as the inside of a flower.

In the valley, all was silent. And clear. And then from far away came a sound of clanking metal. Or that was what Eunhae thought it sounded like as she returned the bones to the ground. She walked a little farther to another spot and started over, digging.

The moon rises and falls . . .

What was the rest of it?

In a moment, Eunhae would remember.

ACKNOWLEDGMENTS

"Bosun" first appeared in *BOMB*. "Cromer" and "Person of Korea" were first published in *The Atlantic*. My deep and profound thanks to the editors who worked so tirelessly and so passionately on these stories.

"At the Post Station" was inspired by Professor Constantine Nomikos Vaporis's *Tour of Duty: Samurai, Military Service in Edo, and the Culture of Early Modern Japan* (University of Hawaii Press, 2008). The generosity and expertise of Professor David L. Howell in the Department of East Asian Languages and Civilizations at Harvard University led me to it. Many details in the story are taken directly from *Tour of Duty*. Others are from Michael J. Seth's *A Concise History of Korea: From Antiquity to the Present* (Rowman & Littlefield, 3rd edition, 2019), which was also an invaluable source for all the stories in this collection.

ACKNOWLEDGMENTS

Numerous details in "The Hive and the Honey" are from *Sakhalin Island* by Anton Chekhov, translated by Brian Reeve (Alma Classics, 2019); *Dersu the Trapper* by V. K. Arseniev, translated by Malcolm Burr (McPherson, 1996); and, most especially, *Sovereignty Experiments: Korean Migrants and the Building of Borders in Northeast Asia, 1860–1945* by Professor Alyssa M. Park (Cornell University Press, 2019).

Alyssa: Thank you—the conceptualization and the writing of so many of the stories in this collection would not have been possible without your scholarship, kindness, and correspondence.

I would also like to thank Professor Terry Martin in the History Department at Harvard University as well as Professor Sergey Glebov in the History Departments at Smith College and Amherst College for their time, knowledge, and goodwill, and for their correspondences on the Russian Far East.

The photographs of Michael Vince Kim were vital to the writing of both "Person of Korea" and "Komarov." The epigraph is from *A Musical Offering* by Luis Sagasti, translated by Fionn Petch (Charco Press, 2020).

Thank you: John Simon Guggenheim Memorial Foundation; Oliver Munday always and forever; *The Atlantic*; Ralph and Gwen Sneeden; Ethan Rutherford and Caroline Casey; Katie Freeman; Yiyun Li and David Means; Andy Tang, Kayley Hoffman, Joal Hetherington, and the team at Simon & Schuster; Marion Duvert, Simon Toop, and all my family at The Clegg Agency.

Laura & Oscar.   Marysue.   Bill.
Thank you for the years.